Bishop

For Pam + Brian Hannah

with the author's
Very Best Regards.
AngusRoss.

## THE LAST ONE

An era is drawing to a close for Marcus Farrow and Charlie McGowan. They have one last assignment—the rescue of Jock McKenzie, being held by the Russians in East Berlin. Farrow's reluctance to be involved any longer in the Game is overcome by a sense of honour, McKenzie having twice saved his life, and by his discovery that McKenzie is the Man's grandson. The problem is, the only possible exchange is with a Russian being held by the Americans who don't want to give him up. So Farrow and Charlie head for Germany, and for a narrow stretch of sea near Travemünde which separates the East from the West, where their last mission ends in a final explosive confrontation.

# THE LAST ONE

**Angus Ross**

CHIVERS PRESS
BATH

First published 1992 by Chivers Press
as a Firecrest Original

0 7451 4409 8

Copyright © Angus Ross, 1992

**British Library Cataloguing in Publication Data available**

Photoset, printed and bound in Great Britain by
Redwood Press Limited, Melksham, Wiltshire

this one is for
Jan and Anita Alexandersson
with love

## AUTHOR'S NOTE

Charlie and I accepted this assignment on Thursday the 17th of November, 1988. But first to live through the events, and later to write any such account—and then to obtain clearance for its publication—involves much wearisome time. Thus, its *raison d'être* has passed into History. Less than one year after these events, the Berlin Wall was seen to crumble almost as rapidly as that which encircled Jericho. For those with an interest in fact, I append a brief chronicle of that phenomenon.

October 18, 1989: The beginning of the end. East German hardline leader Erich Honecker is ousted after thousands flee through Hungary, which had unilaterally opened its borders to the West. New leader Egon Krenz promises reforms, but the mass exodus continues.

November 9: The Berlin Wall suddenly opens. East Germany announces all citizens are free to travel to the West. More than one million do so in the next few days.

November 10: Chancellor Kohl calls for a united Germany. 18 new crossings are opened. Communist Party announces free elections, liberalisation of economy, and scrutiny of its security forces.

November 13: Reformer Hans Modrow chosen as East German Prime Minister, heading new coalition government to include independent parties.

November 20: Over 100,000 East Germans demonstrate in Leipzig for reunification of Germany, removal of Egon K., and for Communist Party to abandon leading role.

November 28: Chancellor Kohl's plan for federation rejected by Egon Krenz and Soviet Union.

December 3: Krenz and Politburo resign.

December 6: Liberal Democrat Manfred Gerlach installed as head of state, ending 40 years of Communist rule.

December 11: First four-power conference for 18 years held to discuss future of Berlin and East Europe.

December 19: Kohl visits East Germany and signs range of agreements. Calls again for 'Unity of our Nation'.

December 22: Brandenburg Gate opened with Kohl and Modrow present. Kohl becomes first West German leader to enter East Berlin.

January 28, 1990: The East's elections brought forward from May 6 to March 18.

January 30: Soviet premier Gorbachev signals guarded acceptance of reunification of Germany.

February 2: Modrow outlines his plan for a united neutral Germany with Berlin as its capital. Kohl, however, opposes neutrality.

February 5: A mob of skinheads goose step through Leipzig yelling *'Sieg Heil!'* at start of regular weekly demonstrations against German unity.

February 7: West German cabinet agrees in principle on currency union with the East, and holds first meeting of 'German Unity' committee.

February 8: West German Justice Ministry working group says Article 23 of Constitution would allow East Germany's five pre-war states to opt to join West Germany's federation.

February 10: East Germany on verge of economic and political collapse as 3,000 of its citizens leave each day, and government authority disintegrates.

February 11 1990: Chancellor Kohl receives Gorbachev's blessing for a united Germany.

So for Charlie and me, this really was the last one. We had long been growing too old for what has been called This Most Dangerous Game. The eternal paradox of sage experience versus youth and vigour.

To survive in the Game, one needs both.

And so, no regrets. It was good while it lasted, but all things come to an end.

A.R., North Yorkshire, 1991.

# TUESDAY

The evening meal was well under way, and I'd supped two preprandial malts, but as I listened to his voice their warm relaxing glow dulled to an icy, creeping chill. I tried several times to interrupt him but, as ever, he took no heed. When at last he paused to allow response:

'Forget it, Charlie,' I said, and I found myself gripping the telephone receiver as though it were Karlin's neck. [See *The Leipzig Manuscript*.] So much for the lovely Glenmorangie, its soothing balm totally annulled. 'And this time, I really do mean it. I've been poorly, I'm not at my best.'

'When were you ever?'

'Flattery gets you nowhere.'

'I promise you, Farrow, this is the last one.'

'Promises, promises,' I said.

'It's very special, it's just for the Man.'

'Oh, sure, so what else is new?'

'I'll tell you what's new, he's fading fast.'

'Aren't we all?' I said, 'but the Man must be well over eighty, so he's had a pretty good run.'

'Listen, idiot! This is important!'

'When was it never?' I said, 'so now say *touché*, and let me get my dinner.'

'Oh, it's "dinner" now, is it?' he said. 'You used to have your dinner at dinner time.'

'That was before I retired, before I became a gentleman of leisure.'

'Gentleman, my arse! Look, I'll see you around half past eight. Be ready.'

'Bollocks,' I said, 'I'm *telling* you, Charlie—'

But I was telling him nothing, because he'd already hung up on me.

\* \* \*

I had planned a special culinary treat. A big thick fillet steak, tender marrow braised in butter, and mushrooms gathered

3

fresh that same day. I'd even put the oven on to bake a couple of spuds, and had opened a half of working man's plonk. For dear old Jake, whose teeth were now few, a pound of tripe simmered in milk with his biscuits softened in the gravy. Splendid scoff indeed, but neither of us enjoyed it. Nothing anthropomorphic, old Jake just sensed my mood. As I cleared away and washed up our dishes, he lay sprawled out on his bed heaving ponderous sighs of sympathy.

'Don't worry, lad,' I said, 'I'm not going to leave you. I'll send the bugger packing.'

He raised his old grey muzzle, then lowered it again, and stiffened his forelegs to let go a special. When the odour permeated my sinuses it seemed redolent of doubt, and disdain. When I went through to build up the sitting-room fire he heaved himself up on four paws and plodded, as always, close to my heels. I switched on the Tv set, glanced briefly at all four programmes, then switched it off again. Nothing worthy of my attention until, perhaps, the nine o'clock news. Before which, and doubtless, Charlie would arrive. The log I'd put on began to take hold and the ruddy, crackling flames were tinged with that iridescent blue which presages a frosty night. A night for settling cosily down with Chopin on the hi-fi, and an oft-read book reinterpreted.

I tried it. No good at all. I couldn't give my mind to Chandler's *Letters*, nor yet to the magic *Berceuse*. Jake snored softly, a-twitched by his dreams. My glances were drawn to the clock, whose metronomic ticking seemed to subjugate the music and to punctuate Raymond's prose. I swear that when I heard the growl of an engine as Charlie slowed to pull into the yard it came as a perverse sort of relief. Jake stirred, and mustered a growl. I lifted a hand, and told him to *stay*, and went to the kitchen door and flicked on the switch for the outside light. He had driven nose-up to the barn, and was climbing out of the Rover. One of the new ones, I saw, and no doubt 'improved' by the Section's mechanics. Same colour, tobacco brown, and him, of course, indigo. Navy blue raincoat, navy blue suit, white shirt, and the old Navy tie. Christ, he might as well carry a

4

placard.

'Where's your dog?' he said. At least he'd remembered I was down to just one.

'Never mind the smooth-talk,' I said, 'you've wasted a journey. I *told* you.'

'Let's get inside. It's cold.'

'It sometimes is, when we get to November.'

'Step aside, then,' he said.

'Now listen, Charlie—'

'Oh, for Christ's sake!'

He brushed me out of his way, and limped across the threshold. I could have impeded him, but after twenty-five years I knew the futility. So:

'How's the leg?' I said.

'You worry about your own leg.'

'All right then, knackers,' I said. I closed the door against a cutting wind, and switched off the outside light. 'But don't take your coat off, because you're not stopping.'

'Get the kettle on,' he said.

I filled the kettle and set it to boil as he took off, and hung up, his coat. Then, a brushing-out of the creases in his Marks & Spencer's suit engendered by sitting in the motor car. A glance at the shine on his shoes, and a smoothing-down of the tight blond waves of his now-receding hair. Followed by a check on the fingernails before he took his spectacles off to polish the rimless lenses on one of his clean handkerchiefs. As he hooked his glasses back over his ears:

'Your flies are undone,' I said.

He didn't look down, he had no need. 'Stop acting the clown,' he said, 'I haven't come here to listen to rhubarb.'

'That's just too bad, Charlie,' I said, 'because rhubarb is all you're going to get. There's a bloody good film on to-night, starts at nine-thirty, right after the news.'

'That kettle's boiling.'

'I know.'

'Well, mash the tea, and mash it strong.'

'Now just a minute—' I said. But he turned away and made for the sitting-room. I reached down a brace of mugs, dumped a tea-bag into each one, and poured boiling water on top. Snarls and growls from the nether regions. 'It's all

5

right, Jake,' I called. 'It's all right, boy, take it easy.'

'Farrow, talk to this hound!'

'What the hell do you think I'm doing? And keep your voice down,' I said, 'you're only upsetting the poor old bugger!' I stirred milk and sugar in the tea, and picked up both mugs and went in to join him. 'You're sitting in my chair.'

'So sit in one of the others.'

'Jesus Christ!' I said. Then, 'That's enough, Jake. Lie down, lie down.'

'Bloody dogs,' Charlie said.

'Charlie, don't push it. Don't push it—okay?' He took a slurp of his tea, laid back his head, and then hunched forwards with his elbows on his knees and both hands clasped round the steaming mug. 'Mate, you look knackered,' I said.

It was true. For the very first time in my life I discerned a change in him and the change was sad, and distressing. It wasn't just his face it was, too, the composition of his body. That marvellous indomitable machine was actually exhibiting signs of fatigue. Only five months ago, in Helmstedt, he had been hit by a couple of slugs either one of which might well have proved fatal.

'Something wrong with the tea?'

'We haven't got much time.'

'We've got plenty of time.'

'No, you don't understand.'

'But I do understand. Forget it, Charlie. Forget it whatever it is.'

'Don't talk nonsense.'

'I am not talking nonsense.'

'It's been a long time,' he said. He was staring into the fireplace.

'Too bloody true,' I said.

'No, I mean since I last saw a fire.'

'That's my whole point,' I said. 'Be serious, old lad. We're past it. We've done our bit, and more. We've played far too long in a young man's game. Leave us let the kids have a go.'

'Kids don't know their arses from their elbows.'

6

'Never did, never will. But it's called the Process of Learning.'

'Don't talk wet,' Charlie said.

'Look, I'm not listening to emotional blackmail, so use young McKenzie,' I said.

'McKenzie's used up. He's been taken.'

'Listen, don't tell me!' I said.

\*    \*    \*

But tell me he did, because that was his purpose.

'. . . come on, they'll swap him,' I said, 'they'll do a swap just like always.'

'To make a swap,' Charlie said, 'you've got to have something worth swapping.'

'So? We must have one of theirs worth at least as much as young Jock McKenzie.'

'Normally, yes,' Charlie said, 'but McKenzie happens to have a famous granddad.'

'Like who?'

'Like the Man,' Charlie said. 'He's the only son of the Man's only daughter, who happens to have been his only child.'

'Charlie, if you're pulling my pisser . . .'

'Give over, Farrow,' he said. 'What the hell do you think this is?'

'Well, you've asked, so I'll tell you,' I said. 'I think we ought to have known from the start.'

'We didn't need to know.'

'Don't feed me *that* old rubbish!'

'What's important now,' he went on, 'is that the Others know whose grandson he is.'

'All the better,' I said. 'It means they'll take bloody good care of him until we nab a big one of theirs.'

'Don't be so stupid! You're giving me a headache!'

We were into our second mug of tea, and the dregs of mine were growing cold. Charlie had hardly touched his, and that was most unusual. In the tea stakes, he was always out front. Even more disturbing was his mention of a headache, and as he massaged his brow I could scarcely believe

7

the evidence of my eyes. Headaches were for ordinary men and I had never, ever, known him to have one.

'Okay, so I'm sorry,' I said, 'so the Man wants to see his grandson once more before he . . .'

'That's right,' Charlie said.

'Where was Jock taken?'

'East Berlin.'

'Oh, Jesus! That's it, then,' I said. 'I'm not going back there. *I am not going back!*'

'Get yourself a drink,' Charlie said.

\*       \*       \*

And—believe this—I needed no second telling, because I could feel myself becoming involved and the feeling was naught for my comfort. I did not wish to know, but I couldn't resist the *knowing*. As I poured myself a jar, Charlie stayed silent, gazing at the fire, and this in itself was enough to prod the worm which stirred in my gut. I took a pull at the malt, but the malt did not render its usual solace. The belly remained unwarmed, and the senses retained a chill morbidity. The undeniable fact was that Charlie and I were dinosaurs in a rapidly-evoluting world. The Section was an anachronism which must surely succumb, with the Man, to historical obscurity. Charlie sighed, and turned his head, and nodded at the drink in my hand.

'Are you ready, now?' he said.

'Ready for what?'

'For listening, for Christ's sake!'

'For listening, yes,' I said.

'Don't be a pillock, I'm tired.'

'Yes, I've noticed,' I said, 'and that's another first in the field.'

'What d'you mean, "first"?' he said.

'I mean, first time I've ever seen you look knackered, and this is the very first time you've ever condoned my having a drink. I'm apprehensive.'

'Balls. You're talking a load of bloody old cods!'

'The "old" part is right,' I said. 'We've grown too old for it, Charlie.'

8

'Speak for yourself,' he said.

'That's exactly what I'm trying to do. I am telling you, my friend, that I am no longer capable of whatever you have in mind.'

'You make me sick, you know that?'

'Lavatory's down the hall.'

'You're asking for it!'

'Asking for what? A slap on the wrist? Leave off!'

'How the hell did I put up with you all these years.'

'You needed me. Simple as that.'

'Always the smart-arse.'

'No, not always. I was a late-developer,' I said.

'Suffering Jesus! Will you shut up, and listen!'

'Sure, I'll listen—but that's all. Then, you want my advice, you're welcome to it.'

'That'll be the day!'

'Not much point in my listening, then.'

'Don't get fancy with me! McKenzie saved your bacon—*twice*.'

'All right, so you counted,' I said, but I couldn't look at him as I said it.

'Damned right I counted,' he said. 'You *owe* him.'

'Emotional blackmail, Charlie.'

'Emotional arseholes!' he said. 'We are talking here about unpaid debts!'

Jake lifted his old grey head, disturbed by the rising level of noise. 'It's all right, Jakie,' I said. Then, 'I doubt if young Jock would see it like that.'

'I don't give a monkey's left tit. We're still going to get him out of Berlin.'

'Not *we*, *you*,' I said. 'So tell me how you propose to do it.'

'Easy. We fix an exchange.'

'I thought you said we'd got nobody to swap?'

'True, I did,' Charlie said, 'but the Cousins are holding a perfect lulu.'

'So what's the problem?' I said.

'They won't play ball.'

'Who won't play ball?'

'The bloody Cousins,' he said. 'They've only just started de-briefing, and they reckon on at least six months.'

9

'Young Jock can sweat that out, easy.'

'Farrow,' Charlie said, 'you stupid bastard, you're missing the point.'

I wasn't, I was just being obtuse. I was trying to blot out a vision of the Man lying on a bed of pain and refusing to let them give him a fix until he'd seen his grandson again.

'We should have been told,' I said. 'We ought to have known about Jock, and the Man.'

'Give over,' Charlie said. 'What bloody difference would it have made?'

'A hell of a lot,' I said. 'I wouldn't have taken him to Hamburg—'

'Bullshit.'

'Say what you like,' I said.

But I *had* always wondered why young Jock McKenzie, last scion of a long noble line and posthumous son of an Arnhem hero and rich beyond avarice had ever chosen to work in the Section. Far from being an élite, the Section had never officially existed. The F.O. it was not. There was never any prospect of any recognition. No ascending ladders to climb. No hope of glory, and no promotion except in the mind of the Man. Never a ribbon to put in the coat, or a stripe to wear on the sleeve, and all remuneration strictly gratuitous. In short, a dead-end job, with all of the emphasis firmly on *dead*.

'It's his own bloody fault, then,' I said. 'Silly young bugger should never have joined.'

'You didn't say that,' Charlie said, 'when he got you out of Travemünde, and Tyneside.'

'He was just doing the job,' I said.

'Exactly.'

'All right, then, so leave it out, Charlie!'

'No chance, Sunshine,' he said. 'I'm going to do it, and you're going to help me.'

'You're going to do what?' I said.

'Take the lulu away from the Cousins.'

'I don't believe it,' I said, 'you can't be serious.'

'Can't I? Why not?'

'It's too bloody crazy!' I said. 'You're talking about stealing a warm live body *from the Cousins*—Jesus Christ! You

10

might as well talk about robbing Fort Knox!'

'Who's Ford Knox?' Charlie said.

'Don't come the old village idiot routine!'

'No, I leave that to you,' Charlie said. 'You're better equipped than I am.'

'So do it without me,' I said. 'Just go away, and leave me alone.'

'If I could, I would,' Charlie said, 'but unfortunately, we're the only ones left.'

'Well, I'm not coming with you,' I said.

*        *        *

We were due to leave Yeadon airport at 22:50 on a commercial flight to Berlin, with a two-hour exchange at Schiphol. Obviously, gone were the days when the Section had its own transport, the lovely HS 125. The Man was laid low, and nothing comes easier than kicking a man when he's down. Five and Six had always hated our guts, and lacking ministerial support, we were always somewhat vulnerable. I suspected then—and still do—that the Section was privately subsidised *ad hoc* from a very privy purse and no prizes for guessing who held the strings.

Niggled by fears for my dog, I shifted my buttocks on the plastic seat, and 'What the hell's going on?' I said. 'They should have called the flight by now.'

'What you worried about?' Charlie said, 'you've got your duty-free rotgut, haven't you?'

'Not the point,' I said.

Three or four feet in front of our faces an enormous window looked out onto acres of neon-lit concrete littered with large aeroplanes, some of them darkened as though in slumber and others, being prepared for the off, plagued by refuelling and maintenance crews. Like calm giants pestered by ants, queen bees crawled all over by drones.

11

# WEDNESDAY

We finally flew out of Schiphol well over an hour adrift, and once we were airborne I nodded off. Charlie roused me with a dig in the ribs as we descended on Tempelhof. Half a city ablaze with lights, the other half shrouded in relative darkness. I had the window seat. I looked down onto the sprawl of suburbs as we banked to make the approach, and picked out that old familiar landmark. The floodlit Soviet Army War Memorial, situated on several prime acres of East Berlin real estate, makes Nelson's Column look like a matchstick. As the pilot banked east and south the miserable River Spree was visible only in stretches, overshadowed by the Wall and the endless blocks of dreary tenements which crowded its opposite bank. No great soaring arches of bridges such as those between Buda and Pest, or even as those which link north and south London.

I yawned, and rubbed my eyes. It was getting on for three in the morning, the middle of a wearisome night, and I yearned again for my own warm bed. A stewardess came round offering boiled sweets to ward off ear-blockage. Charlie waved her away, and we heard the thumping of undercarriage locks and the peevish whining of flaps. Just one gentle bump as we made a smooth landing, then the banshee howling of jets as the pilot reversed engine thrust. The taxiing seemed to take forever, but Customs and Immigration were an absolute piece of cake. I did not know, and I couldn't have cared less, whether any word had been passed. All I cared about, then, was adopting a horizontal position between a pair of clean sheets.

An icy shiver as we stepped out of the concourse was not entirely due to the cold. 'I hope we're not hanging about for the bus.'

'We'll get a cab,' Charlie said.

Amazing. I'd expected an argument. 'Thank God. Where to, then?' I said.

'We're stopping at the Hilton.'

'Never!'

'Don't get carried away,' Charlie said.

*     *     *

See one Hilton, you've seen 'em all. They do a fair old breakfast, though. As I broke the yolk of my second egg:

'How much longer?' Charlie said.

'Have a heart, I've only just started!'

'Shake it up, then,' he said. 'My room in ten minutes.'

'Make it fifteen.'

'Look, don't hang about,' he said.

'Scout's honour,' I said, through a mouthful of bacon.

'Bloody disgusting,' he said.

I joined him twenty minutes later prepared for the usual blast, and felt curiously uneasy when it didn't materialise. He was definitely slowing down. Good in one way, very bad in another. He was sitting on the bed, having just put down the telephone receiver.

'Right then, Charlie,' I said, 'what's all the panic?'

'Don't get sat down, just pin your ears back. We've a meet on the other side—' he held up a hand as I opened my mouth '—and don't pee your britches, 'cos it's all above board. We're going to see Bernhard Schwenk.'

'Isn't he the geezer who—'

'Yes, he is. He'll be representing both sides.'

It came as no great surprise. Herr Doktor Schwenk was, and probably still is, a famous legal eagle whose sole apparent mission in life was to act as a human-being-broker. He was the middleman with friends in high places on either side of the Wall, and his fees were said to be astronomical. His fees from the West, that is. No-one ever knew what the Others paid him. Most likely nothing at all.

'That bastard will want a king's ransom, Charlie.'

'That's none of our business,' he said. 'Our job's to make sure that it all goes smoothly.'

'You mean, see that we're not double-crossed. But where do the Cousins come in?'

'They don't. Not so far as Schwenk's concerned. All *he* needs to know is who we have for swapping.'

'Oh, well, that's easy,' I said, '—except that we don't have

13

a *who* to offer.'

'Not yet. So you keep your big mouth shut, and let me do all the talking.'

'Hey, listen, feel free!' I said.

\*   \*   \*

It was chilly but bright, a fine Autumn morning and the well-preserved shell of the Gedächtniskirche at the junction of Tauentzienstrasse and the big throbbing Kurfürstendamm seemed to bask in the bonus sunlight. There are those who sneer at the monument, but I am not one of them. To me, it stands as an admonition, it symbolises the rape of Berlin.

Schwenk had sent his car to collect us. None of your Russian crap, a bloody great black Mercedes with quite enough room in the back for a game of five-a-side football. The driver sat up front in a private playground all to himself. He took the road alongside the canal which runs up to Hallesches Tor U-bahn station, heading for the checkpoint on Friedrichstrasse.

'Have the passport ready,' Charlie said.

That which he'd given me before we left home—Christ! Was it just yesterday?—identified me as one Edmund Foster, of Richmond in Yorkshire. Occupation, business consultant. Could mean anything.

'I hope it's a proper Foreign Office job.'

'Stop worrying,' Charlie said, 'they're not going to give a monkey's.'

As it turned out, he was right. But that didn't stop me from sweating when we stopped at the barrier pole and a shit-faced little vopo with a Schmeisser at the alert stepped up to Charlie's wound-down window. Charlie never said a word. He just handed over the dicky passports with a knowing nod at the youth, and settled back and said:

'See? I told you.'

'Yeah, I know,' I said, 'but we're not through yet, and we've got to get back.'

'One thing I hate, it's a lack of faith.'

'Never mind lack of faith. Did it ever occur to you that it

14

might be *us* they really want?'

'Bullshit,' Charlie said, and he shot a furious warning glance at the back of our driver's head.

Seconds passed like minutes, and minutes passed like hours. Two cars in front and another behind were emptied of passengers, all of whom were shepherded into the hut to sit out the processing bit. It couldn't have been more than three or four minutes before our own particular vopo emerged with a marked relaxing of the facial muscles. He even mustered a smile as he handed back our passports. Our chauffeur, as though it were routine, trundled us smoothly across the flat bridge and into the Eastern zone. Last time I'd crossed, it had been rather less easy. I breathed a sigh of relief, and contracted my armpits to mop up the sweat.

'Farrow,' Charlie said, 'you ought to use a deodorant.'

'Knackers. Get stuffed,' I said.

*       *       *

It is wrong to make judgements on first impressions, but my first impression of Schwenk was that of a bloated gastropod. Fat, he certainly was. He had a belly like the bows of a barge. He must have weighed three hundred pounds, about five of which were composed of chins exclusive of wattles, and smile. The hand he extended across his huge desk looked for all the world like a bunch of anaemic bananas. Charlie ignored it.

'So.' Schwenk sank back, an amorphous mass in his oversized captain's chair, and waved away the spinsterish female who had diffidently ushered us in. 'Please be seated, gentlemen.'

'No thanks, we'll stand,' Charlie said, hands thrust deep into raincoat pockets. I adopted a similar pose, and tried to look inscrutable.

'Introduce your friend,' Schwenk said. His smile was as oily as a tin of sardines.

'He's not my friend,' Charlie said, 'I hardly know him. Let's get to the business.'

'Ah, yes, the business,' Schwenk said. His desk top, big

15

enough to land-on a Swordfish, was absolutely bare except for a huge hide-bound blotter on which lay a slim cardboard file. He opened its stiff green cover and pretended to scan the first page through his shiny gold-rimmed half-lenses. 'Jason Heald,' he went on, 'also known as Hector McKenzie, also—'

'All right,' Charlie said, 'never mind the curriculum vitae, just make sure that we get the right man.'

'Of that there can be no possible question, but my clients in the East have expressed a doubt as to whether you can produce the party of the second part.'

I liked that. *Party of the second part.*

'That's *our* problem,' Charlie said.

'Might one enquire how you mean to resolve it?'

'No, one might not,' Charlie said.

'When will you be ready to effect the exchange?'

'Within about a week. We'll give you twenty-four hours notice.'

'That is not enough. There are delicate negotiations—'

'Rubbish,' Charlie said, 'we are talking here about a one-for-one. A simple, straightforward swap.'

'Nevertheless—'

'Stop farting around. Piss, or get off the pot.'

Schwenk steepled his bunches of bananas, elbows on the arms of his chair, and looked at Charlie over the tops of his glasses. 'My dear sir, really!' he said. His accent, in English, was vaguely American. 'Such language!'

'Balls,' Charlie said, 'we didn't come here to be messed about. We want a yes, or a no. If it's *no*, we'll get ourselves another pimp, one who can handle the job.'

Schwenk's heavy jowls assumed the same hue as those of a turkey cock, but he kept control. His voice remained steady.

'I must warn you—'

'Bugger off,' Charlie said. His right hand emerged from his raincoat pocket and a big fat envelope fell with a thud on Schwenk's blotter. The fat man glanced down at it, and then looked up into Charlie's eyes. 'Cash in advance,' Charlie said, 'fifty thousand, American.' He rested his knuckles on the edge of Schwenk's desk and leaned across its top until

16

their faces were only inches apart. 'Now, that is a lot of *Geld*, so make sure you earn it because if you don't, you are *dead*.' He straightened up. 'And that is a promise.'

'Gentlemen, goodbye,' Schwenk said.

\*       \*       \*

Europe's longest, straightest, and widest urban thoroughfare—and, once, its most beautiful—can't make up its mind what it wants to be called. Successive stretches have different names but the first, running West from the city centre, is known all over the world: the one and only Unter den Linden, spanned by the Brandenburg Gate and also by the border which divides Berlin. The second leg of its eighteen kilometres runs through the Tier and Zoo Gartens having adopted the unlovely name Strasse des 17 Juni. This changes at Ernst-Reuter-Platz to Bismarck Strasse, which changes to Kaiser Damm, which at Theodor Heuss becomes Heer Strasse. This last runs all the way up to and beyond the city limits. After sailing through the checkpoint in Schwenk's great *Strassekruezer* we veered left to cross a loop of the Spree and then to cross 17 Juni. I looked down the Unter den Linden towards the Brandenburg Gate. Over there, them: on this side, us. Christ, what an obscenity.

Raucous traffic swarmed all around the Merc like flies round an elephant, but the car's vast interior was quiet as the grave. Not once since leaving the lawyer's office had Charlie spoken a word, but when Schwenk's driver dropped us at the Hilton, 'Settle the bills,' he said, 'and then get your gear, we're leaving.'

'I thought it was too good to be true.'

'Well, now you know.'

'Okay, but what do I use for money?'

'Use the credit card,' he said.

Most unusual. Emergencies apart, we never used credit cards except as a provenance, as one of the standard items in a false identity kit. Plastic credit is recorded on computers and, as everyone knows, computers can as easily be made to cough up their secrets as a Piccadilly whore drops her drawers. Had Phileas Fogg used a credit card on his eighty-day trip round the world, a smart technician could have monitored his progress *ahead* of his next port of call. Believe this, people, and think on that prospect.

'Well, you're the boss,' I said, 'but the Others will know before I've done signing.'

'I don't give a monkey's chuff.'

*       *       *

We left Am Zoo station on a stopping train to Wannsee, with a change at Zehlendorf. The fast trains don't stop until they reach the border at nearby Griebnitzsee. Freibad Wannsee, a waterfront village pretty enough to break your heart, lies at the bottom end of the Havel, a lake about ten miles long running almost parallel with the East/West border. To the beleaguered denizens of Berlin, it represents the seaside. It is cruised by pleasure boats, and there are makeshift beaches and islands with castles. This late in the season, though, it was one of the most fine and private places in the whole of West Berlin, and I'd have preferred the anonymity of crowds.

'I don't like this, Charlie,' I said. 'I feel eyes on my backbone.'

'What backbone?'

'Up yours also,' I said.

We had left our baggage at the station and were standing on the landing stage watching one of Bruno Winkler's boats, the *Vaterland*, making fast alongside. We were waiting together with about forty others to embark on a cruise of the lake, and incoming passengers were crowding the rails all ready to step back on shore. Over on the opposite side of the lake, that which lay in the DDR, a gloomy forest of pines looked impenetrable.

Those disembarking seemed predominantly American, ageing ex-GIs paying valedictory homage to those halcyon days of their youth when they rampaged here as conquering heroes. As they straggled towards their waiting coach, I overheard one of the wives complaining.

'We should of had lunch on the boat.'

'We're all gonna eat at the ho-*tel* fachrissakes!'

18

Most of our fellow passengers made straight for the open upper deck, all the better to see the sights.

'Let's get down the back,' Charlie said.

'You mean, the stern.'

'I mean the back.'

'Please yourself,' I said.

When she joined us a few minutes later, 'Hello, Edna,' Charlie said, 'long time no see. This is Farrow.' He let us exchange how-d'ye-dos, and then went on, 'Did you spot any limpets?'

'No, you're clean,' she said.

'Are you sure?'

'Do you want it in writing?'

'Attagirl, Edna,' I said.

'Farrow, why don't you go take a walk?'

'How's the Old Man?' Edna said. 'Word has it here that he's on his last legs.'

'He's hanging on,' Charlie said, 'until we get this lot over.'

'Him and me both,' Edna said. 'I'm packing it in, I've had enough.'

'Goes for all of us,' Charlie said.

I added my silent but heartfelt agreement. Edna was a little old bird, couldn't have weighed much more than a sparrow. Dark green *loden* coat, pork-pie hat with a breast feather in it. Short-cropped gunmetal hair, eyes like wet jet buttons. Tiny delicate hands, liver-spotted but still smooth and shapely. A beauty, in her day, without any possible rissom of doubt. I wondered about her, and the Man. The Section was always full of surprises. Dangerous, but never dull. We were leaning with forearms flat on the stern-rail, staring down at the roiling wake. Beside us, Edna looked child-like and frail. Believe that, believe anything.

'They're holding our boy at Blankenburg.' A suburb of north East Berlin.

'So it looks like they're ready to do business,' said Charlie.

'Looks like it, yes,' Edna said. 'But I'm telling you, laddo, you'd better be careful.'

'You know me,' Charlie said.

'Yes, but there's always a first time, old love.'

19

*Old love?* What the hell was going on? I felt like the proverbial spare at a wedding, so maybe I *should* take that walk. But I didn't, I stayed to play gooseberry. There was a stiffish breeze off the lake. I pondered on the absence of scavenging gulls.

'. . . so I take it, then,' Charlie said, 'that the Cousins are still holding Dorf in Frankfurt.'

'Of course, where else?' Edna said. 'I've brought you two tickets for the five o'clock flight.'

'Good. Did you contact the girl?'

'Yes, I gave her a ring before I left home.'

'That's fine. So let's talk about you. How long have you been here in this foreign field?'

'Quite long enough,' Edna said. 'So you get your skates on, and let's all go home.'

'Amen, Edna,' I said.

\*　　　\*　　　\*

It was growing dark when we landed at Frankfurt, and apart from a snack on the boat I'd had nothing to eat since that Hilton breakfast. I wanted some decent scoff, and a nice hot bath, and a nice quiet read, and then perchance to dream. What I got was something quite different.

'Now then,' Charlie said, as we stood by the slow-moving carousel waiting for our bags to appear, 'when we get outside look for Ursula.'

'Ursula? Who's Ursula?' I said.

'Christ! Has the booze destroyed *all* of your brain cells?'

'You don't mean—'

'I do,' he said.

'But she's one of Schumacher's lot! And after what we did to Willy . . .'

'Forgiven, and forgotten,' Charlie said. 'Willy needed a very big favour.'

'I can't believe it. Are you trying to tell me—'

'Our gear's coming up,' he said, 'so get it off, and let's get moving.'

'You crippled or something?' I said, and as soon I'd said it I could have bitten my tongue off. I noticed dark rings round

20

his eyes, and lines on his face indicative of pain. So I hauled our bags off the belt and lugged them, lop-sided, after him. He was limping heavily. Charlie, limping. An icy fist closed in my chest, and I almost dropped the cases I was carrying. He had always been my rod and my staff, my omnipresent sheet-anchor. Tagging after him now, through the press of travellers thronging the concourse, I was seized by a feeling of dread. I bullied my way through some camera-bedecked Japanese tourists and, 'Hang *on* a minute!' I said.

He looked back over his shoulder and, 'Come on, Farrow!' he said, 'what the hell are you moaning about?'

'Look, I'm not a bloody pack-horse,' I said.

Frankfurt airport. So very evocative with its old aeroplanes strung from the roof and an imagined odour of beer and sauerkraut. Hard vinyl tiles underfoot, and a powerful ambience of *déjà vu*. Incongruously, I thought of my dog, and then the sheer weight of Charlie's suitcase forced me to put it down and switch it from left hand to right hand. Ahead, the automatic doors had swished open as he approached them. 'Hang on!' I shouted again.

He took no notice. The doors closed, then opened again, and I followed him out into a drizzle of rain. I wished I was somewhere else. It was a wretched miserable evening, damp and cold and drear, with encroaching night bringing thin wet mist.

'Let me help you,' Ursula said.

She was only a lass, but I let her help me because she was young and strong and I felt old and weary and his suitcase weighed a ton. Between us, we heaved it into the boot and then she hopped in up front and I slumped into the back beside Charlie. As we drew away, Ursula looked up into her mirror.

'So. You are back,' she said.

It was a statement rather than a question. 'Yes, we're back,' Charlie said. 'No hard feelings?'

'No hard feelings.'

'That's the style. What's the point?' Charlie said. Then, 'Where are we staying?'

'At my place.'

'Is it safe?'

21

'Who knows?' the girl said, 'but there are many hotels in Frankfurt, so if you'd rather—'

'No, no,' Charlie said, 'so long as we won't be putting you out.'

'No problem,' Ursula said.

Sitting there in her little Volkswagen, I felt like a pawn in the game. She was an expert, skilful driver. She ploughed through the airport shit, and soon we were on the back road to Kronberg. I remembered it only too well. I also remembered our little chauffeuse. Oh, to be young again. In another time, and another place . . . But anyway, what the hell. The rapture can never be recaptured. This kid was like beautiful. A shapely head most marvellously adorned by close-cut copper-glinting curls and a figure, though slim, with gut-wrenching curves. Quite small but gorgeous tits, and a smile enhanced by perfect teeth. I knew why she did this job, but what a waste. What a bloody waste.

'And how are *you*, Nelson?' she said.

'Don't mind me. I'm just here for the ride.'

'Oh, yes, I'm sure,' she said. Her English was perfect, and idiomatic.

'So what's the score?' Charlie said.

'They're keeping Dorf in the Army barracks.'

'Jesus Christ,' Charlie said.

'But we have a friend.'

'What kind of friend?'

'Well, an ally, then,' Ursula said. 'Sergeant Kramer, one of Dorf's keepers. We caught him in a honey trap, and now he's ours until he's posted back home.'

'Naughty,' Charlie said. 'If the Cousins find out, they'll crucify you.'

'Oh, he hasn't been much use—until now.'

'So you reckon he's pretty reliable?'

'Yes, we do,' the girl said. 'We have him by the, er . . .'

'Short and curlies?'

She laughed delightedly. 'I was trying to think of *scruff of the neck*. But your phrase is better, Herr Nelson.'

'Call me Farrow,' I said. ' "Nelson" was only for Leipzig.'

'How's your boss?' Charlie said.

'Herr Schumacher's fine.'

'Not nursing a grudge?'

'Oh no, no,' Ursula said. 'In fact, I think he rather admires you.'

'That's a comfort,' Charlie said.

It was more than a comfort, it was a minor miracle. When we'd all worked together to get Vogel out of Leipzig they had tried a double-cross, but Charlie was one step ahead of Willy and we'd left him with jam on his face. A lot of jam. Very messy.

'And how's young Eberhardt?' I said. Eberhardt had made up the trio of their team.

Ursula dropped two gears to shoot us past a lumbering juggernaut. The way she carved up the truck caused an urgent constriction of the sphincter muscle, but she handled the car so well that the twitching soon subsided.

'Eberhardt has left us,' she said, 'for a career which offers greater . . . security.'

'You mean life-expectancy,' I said.

'Farrow—'

'Yes, Charlie?'

'Shut your cake-hole.'

'No, let him speak,' the girl said. 'You are in my car, and this is my country.'

'Doesn't matter. Forget it,' I said.

None of us bothered to talk after that. It was cosy inside the car, and the weather outside seemed worlds away. Ursula made excellent time, and was soon turning onto the short steep hill on the outskirts of Kronberg 2 on which her flat was situated. There were parking spaces out front. She braked, and reversed into one of them, then switched the engine off and turned her head to look over her shoulder.

'Home sweet home,' she said.

'Get the bags then, Farrow.'

'Let me get out first!' I said.

Ursula's apartment was big enough for two but for three, unless two were sleeping partners, it was not quite big enough. It posed a slight problem of who kipped where. There was one big double bed, and a convertible couch in the sitting room, but although two and two make four, three singles do not make two doubles. Ursula insisted that we

23

use the bedroom.

'Right, then,' Charlie said, 'I'll take the bed.'

'Great, but what about me?'

'What's wrong with the floor?' Charlie said. 'There's a sleeping bag here, and plenty of blankets. You've slept in worse places.'

'True. But shouldn't we toss a coin, or something?'

'Chain of command.'

'Piss off!'

But it was only a token objection. I was worried about the old sod. I'd never before ever known him look ill but now he looked tired and worn, and I selfishly feared for my own protection.

'All right, then, but listen,' I said, 'do *not* wake me up to tell me I'm snoring. I want to go early to bed, and I want a nice long undisturbed kip.'

'You must be joking,' he said.

Ursula was out in her neat little kitchen, rustling up a quick meal. It wasn't Egon Ronay, but it filled a gap. As Ursula and I sipped a postprandial coffee—Charlie drank only water, or tea—he said:

'Come on, it's time we were off.'

'Can't we wait and see Willy tomorrow morning?'

'No, we bloodywell can't. Get your coat on, make a move.'

'Lovely meal, Ursula,' I said, 'but it looks like we have to love you and leave you.'

'No. I'm coming, too,' she said.

\*   \*   \*

The US Army barracks in Frankfurt, HQ of the American zone, are reckoned to be invulnerable. Secure from terrorist attack, and impervious to demo mobs. They scared the shit out of me, Sergeant Kramer or no Sergeant Kramer. Ursula drove us past, then went around the block and drove past again.

'Guard house well-manned,' Charlie said.

'Yes,' said Ursula, 'and the guards use real bullets.'

'And it's a bloody big place,' I said. 'An awful lot of

24

buildings.'

'Stop wetting yourself,' Charlie said. Then, to the girl, 'How far from the fence?'

'About two hundred metres,' she said.

'Christ! That's just about two hundred too many!'

'Ignore him,' Charlie said. He was sitting up front, with the wipers clacking, and me crouched forwards in the back. As we made a second pass of the barracks, 'This Kramer geezer,' he said, 'are you absolutely sure of him?'

'Positively,' Ursula said. 'So long as he's covered, he'll do what we ask.'

'Listen, lass,' Charlie said, 'we are talking here about something *vital*.'

'I know.'

'Well, so long as you know,' Charlie said, 'you can take us, now, to your leader.'

'He's waiting for us,' Ursula said.

*       *       *

The house was way out in the boondocks, on Frankfurt's rural fringe. Secluded, but not conspicuously so. It stood in a half-acre of ground hedged, like its neighbours, with fast-growing cypresses. There was a double garage at one side with, parked in front, a big BMW. As Ursula drew up alongside I thought I detected a shift in the shadows created by the dim yellow light from a pair of carriage lamps which flanked the front porch. Ursula's brief stab on the bell was answered so quickly I knew we were expected. Schumacher opened the door.

'*Wie geht's*, Charles?'

'Speak English, Willy.'

'Of course—come in, come in!'

He stood aside to let us enter, and as I passed him he nodded at me. 'And how is Mr Nelson?'

'Bearing up. How's yourself?' I said.

Him and Charlie were physical twins. Same deceptive build, and the same smooth body action. Extremely lithe, and fit. He looked about forty, but was closer to sixty. No hint of grey in his hair which was short and thick, the colour

25

of strong tea, same colour as hooded eyes set rather close together across a bold jut of nose. Wide thin lips and a good strong chin. A face which said *nemo me impune lacessit*. But we *had* injured him, and we'd injured him where it hurt most: his pride. If he still bore a grudge, he was hiding it well.

'Please—take off your coats, and sit down.'

Safe houses have a smell about them, that indefinable air of transitory occupation experienced in remote hotels. Of furniture and furnishings unloved and uncared for, old chairs with wooden arms only slightly less resilient than their lumpy upholstery. It was warm to the point of discomfort, the heating too fast and too much. As I began to unbutton my raincoat:

'Don't take it off,' Charlie said, 'we'll only be here a few minutes.'

'Same old Charles,' Willy said. 'But do sit down.'

'Get on with it, then.' Charlie took his spectacles off, and fished out one of his clean handkerchiefs. 'Kramer.'

'Ah, yes, of course,' Willy said. 'I see that our Ursula has briefed you on the sergeant.'

'Let's hear it from you,' Charlie said.

'He will be on duty on Thursday night, starting at 8 p.m.'

'What about his buddies?'

'Two others, and Kramer is in charge.'

'In charge of what?'

'The guard at one of the houses in the officers' quarters. Dorf is being softened up. He is not being held in the cell blocks, Charles.'

'But it's two hundred yards from the fence.'

'Roughly, two hundred metres.'

'Same difference,' Charlie said.

'He's been there three weeks. The Americans have grown careless.'

'Listen,' Charlie said, 'don't underestimate the Cousins.'

'Americans!' Schumacher sneered, 'the sweepings-up of disaffected nations!'

'Including yours,' Charlie said.

'We are not here to talk about past history.'

'Too bloody true,' Charlie said, 'but it was you who

started it—wasn't it, Farrow?' He said it without looking at me. He never took his eyes off Willy.

'Definitely,' I said, 'but it seems to me—'

'And it seems to me,' he said, 'that you need some fresh air. So take your little friend for a walk in the garden.'

'Give over, it's raining!' I said.

'So take an umbrella.'

'There is one in the hall.'

'Come on, Ursula,' I said.

But we didn't go outside, we sat in the kitchen. Every conceivable mod con, but hardly any of them ever used. She plugged in the coffee pot, and then began to open cupboards.

'I am looking for bottles,' she said, 'because I think that now you might also like some whisky.'

'Don't bother, lass,' I said. 'I can take it or leave it.'

'Ah! Here we are!'

'Well, go on, then,' I said.

Her simple dress of soft brown wool moulded her unfettered breasts and clung to her waist and the swell of her hips. She smelled very cleanly of soap, with an overtone of some subtle perfume. As she leaned over me to pour out a goodly measure of whisky the impulse to reach out and clasp was almost irresistible. I think she sensed my urge, because as she straightened up she patted my back and said with a grin in her voice, 'Drink up, and relax. You look somewhat tired.'

'Don't let that fool you,' I said.

She took a seat across the table, and, 'So,' she said with a smile, 'I suppose I had better take care of myself!'

'Joking apart,' I said, 'I hope you're not going to be actively involved.'

'Oh yes. I am,' she said.

'We'll see about that.'

'It is seen to already.' She leaned forward to touch my hand and her fingers, though warm, sent a shiver up my arm.

'Hey listen, just watch it!' I said, and we were both still laughing when Charlie appeared.

'Right then, we're off,' he said. Willy Schumacher was

standing behind him.

'Just a minute,' I said, 'Ursula's just told me—'

'*I'm* telling you we're leaving.'

'*Guten Nacht, Ursula,*' Schumacher said.

*       *       *

In the car, as Ursula drove us back to her flat, 'You've been drinking,' Charlie said, 'you smell like a barmaid's apron.'

'Never mind about that,' I said. 'I'm worried about this kid—'

'She's not a kid.'

'I still don't want her involved.'

'She's all grown up. She knows her own mind.'

Ursula drove the car as though totally deaf to all we were saying.

'Be that as it may be,' I said, 'she's still just a lass.'

'She's a woman, and Women's Lib Rules—okay?'

'No, it's not okay. I don't like it.'

'Think of the Greenham bunch.'

'You call that lot *women*? Jesus, they didn't know up from down! Most of 'em were in it for the old slap-and-tickle!'

'Same thing.'

'Nothing of the kind. This is entirely different.'

'We need her,' Charlie said.

'What you mean is, we need to use her.'

'Farrow, don't get smart.'

'Balls. I'm ahead of you, Charlie.'

'That'll be the day.'

'So you keep telling me.'

'I'm telling you again. You know what your problem is? You've never been anything but an amateur.'

'Oh, sure, and thank God,' I said. 'Means I don't go around with blinkers on?'

'Blinkers, bollocks,' he said, 'you want to learn to think positive.'

'Well, we're both still around, and if I hadn't thought positive—'

'Don't kid yourself.'

'Oh, hell, what's the use?' I said.

The residents' parking slots were all occupied, so Ursula turned the car onto the blacktop area belonging to the church on the opposite side of the road. The darkness was tranquil, and still. No feeling of threat, and no sense of danger. Clouds streaked the face of the moon but its light, though diffused, remained sufficient to see us across the way. Ursula fished keys from out of her handbag, and: '*Scheisse!* It's cold!' she said.

As we walked down the path on the side of the block to the back and only door, Charlie said, 'Not so fast, hang on . . .'

'What's your problem?' I said, 'Let's get inside, it's freezing out here.' Midnight had come and gone, and the only lights in the six-unit block were those in a top-floor flat from which came faint noise of idiot music. A party going on. All I wanted was to get to bed. '*Liebchen*, open the door.'

Charlie said, 'Hang on a minute.'

'Hey, come *on*, Chas!' I said.

Her key poised, Ursula hesitated.

'All right, go ahead,' Charlie said.

So Ursula unlocked the outer door, and then the door to her flat, and when she switched the lights on:

'About time,' Westerholme said. 'Permit me to introduce my colleagues.'

'Don't bother,' Charlie said. 'We don't wish to know them—do we, Farrow?'

'Not especially,' I said.

They were sitting, three of them, in Ursula's sitting-room, ranged around the sofa-bed. The other two had guns in their fists.

'Look at 'em,' Charlie said, 'bloody pathetic.'

'I quite agree, Charles. I'm ashamed of you, Westerholme,' I said.

'That don't make me no beeswax.'

'Farrow?'

'Rough translation,' I said, 'means he doesn't give a monkey's.'

'I see.' Charlie seemed quite unperturbed. He took off, and shook out, his raincoat, and pushed his glasses up on his nose and smoothed down his hair and seated himself on

29

the one remaining chair, and adjusted the creases of his trousers. Preparing to enjoy himself.

'It might also be interpreted—'

'Yes, thank you, Farrow.'

'Don't mention it,' I said.

Westerholme heaved a heavy sigh. He knew from more than one previous experience that we were taking the piss out of him, and that nothing he could do might stop us. Westerholme was CIA, of the up-and-coming new generation, one of the few Company men for whom I had any sort of respect. We had first come up against him when he was just a minor cog in the wheel which was turning, at that time, in Luxembourg. Now, he was patently In Charge, symbol of a fast-changing hierarchy.

Charlie was not impressed. He sat back, and put his fingertips together, and 'Unburden yourself, Westerholme,' he said. 'You've got just one minute to spit it out.'

And they were the ones with the guns.

'Now listen, McGowan—'

'*Mister* McGowan.'

'They've no manners, Charlie,' I said.

'Westerholme's upset. He's got something on his mind.'

'You are very damn right!' Westerholme said. 'When you two jokers get together right here in our own backyard—'

'*Your* backyard? I thought it was Germany's.'

'Come off it, you know what I mean!'

'We're on holiday, aren't we, Farrow?'

'First for a long time,' I said. 'We're only here for the beer, Wes.'

'McGowan doesn't drink,' he said.

'Whatever gave you that idea? He's a noted connoisseur of the hop—that right, Charlie?'

'Right as rain.'

'There you go,' I said, 'you have it straight from the horse's mouth.'

'Bullshit!' Westerholme said. 'You bastards are up to something!'

'Not true,' Charlie said. 'I'll have you know that my parents were married.'

30

'Mine, too, Charlie,' I said. 'Wes wants to watch his language.'

'Jesus!' Westerholme said.

'See what I mean, Chas?'

'I do indeed. These poor colonials, though, we must allow them a certain latitude.'

'Well, up to a point,' I said, 'but there *is* a limit, Charlie. They've had two hundred years to learn.'

'Perhaps they're just late-developers.'

'Perhaps, but even so . . .'

'We mustn't be too hard on them, Farrow.'

'That's all very well,' I said, 'but I didn't come here to be insulted.'

'So why *did* you come?' Westerholme said.

'As a matter of fact, we're just passing through.'

'So pass through,' Westerholme said, 'and don't forget we'll be watching you.'

'You couldn't watch Tv.'

'You think so?'

'We know so.'

'We traced you here.'

'Rhubarb,' Charlie said. 'You had your people stationed at the airport, they saw the girl pick us up, so you simply came here, and waited.'

'Brilliant.'

'Elementary,' Charlie said. 'We expected you—didn't we, Farrow?'

'As night follows day,' I said. 'So now, if you'll excuse us . . .'

'No way!' Westerholme said. 'We know you've got to be here for *something*!'

'What a shame it is,' I said, 'that our world should be plagued by fear and suspicion.'

'Lamentable,' Charlie said.

'An absence of faith in human nature.'

'Sad, but true,' Charlie said. 'I can hardly believe this is happening.'

'No more can I,' I said. 'I'd always assumed we were partners.'

'So we are,' Charlie said.

31

'No, I don't mean *us*, I mean us and them.'

'Jesus!' Westerholme said.

'Our friend seems to have a limited vocabulary.'

'Well, Yale isn't Oxford,' I said. 'It thinks it is, but it's a long way to go.'

'Cut the shit!' Westerholme said. His minders were sitting there with brows all furrowed, still with guns in their hands, looking from one to another of us. Ursula was equally bemused, standing beside me beside the door. 'You, Farrow, take a chair!'

'There isn't one.'

'So sit on the bed!'

'Wes, I'm old. I need a back-rest.'

One of the goons with guns laughed and said, 'He needs a back-rest!'

'Shut up,' Westerholme said. 'And for Christ's sake put those things away.' I sensed he was beginning to have doubts, and as pistols were tucked away under armpits, 'All right, then,' he went on, 'what's the score? What brings you to Frankfurt?'

'I told you,' Charlie said, 'we're passing through on our way down to München. This is just an overnight stop.'

'Any particular reason for it?'

'Listen, Westerholme,' I said, 'you mind your business, and we'll mind ours.'

'What he means,' Charlie said, 'is he wanted to visit his girlfriend *en route*.'

Ursula caught on fast, and responded with well-performed protest. 'Girl friend? No!' she said, 'Herr Farrow is old enough to be my father!'

'Oh, thank you, Ursula,' I said.

'My *mother* was his girl friend!'

And there was enough veracity in that to persuade any sceptic she was telling the truth, and it is ever upon such small truths that the biggest lies are afforded credence. Westerholme shot me a grin which might also have been described as a leer.

'Why, you dirty old man, you,' he said.

'Look, you've got it all wrong!'

'Leave it, Farrow.'

32

'Never mind "leave it"!' I said, 'this bugger's hinting—'

'So let him hint.'

'I'll remember this, Westerholme,' I said.

'I said to forget it,' said Charlie.

'Bugger that for a tale!', and now I was only half-acting, 'Wes, I'll remember this!'

'So hold it against me.'

'You'd better believe it!'

'Gentlemen,' Charlie said, 'we're departing from the point in question.'

'Right on!' one of the goons said. Charlie ignored the interruption.

'So, if that's all,' he went on, 'we will bid you an overdue Sailor's Farewell.'

When his minions had shouldered their guns, I'd felt oddly embarrassed for Westerholme. He was quite a considerable man, and he didn't need this kind of help to pass a message on. He could just as effectively have come alone. He seemed to sense my thoughts. He looked away as I sought his eyes, and coughed to clear his throat, but just as I made a mental decision to stop my needling of him, Charlie said:

'That's a pretty bad cough. You shouldn't be out in this cold night air, laddie.'

'A wise guy,' the youngest goon said.

Westerholme flashed him a look of dismissal, and pushed himself up on his feet. 'All right, let's go.'

'Oh, *must* you?' said Charlie. 'Miss Uhde, show them out.'

Westerholme let the others precede him, then paused in the doorway, and turned. 'Don't try to drop out of sight, we'll find you.'

'Give over,' Charlie said, 'I doubt if you can find your way back to Frankfurt.'

After they were gone, Ursula said, 'I'll make us some coffee.'

'Make mine tea,' Charlie said. 'I hope you've got plenty of hot water?'

'Yes, lots.'

'Thank God for that,' I said.

33

As we spoke he was making urgent signals with a finger across his lips. I cottoned on fast, and so did the girl.

'They didn't believe you,' she said, 'they didn't believe you were on your way to München.'

'All the better,' I said.

'But the double bluff is a two-edged sword.'

'Exactly,' Charlie said.

'But they might decide to follow you down to München.'

'In which case,' Charlie said, 'we'll have made them split forces. Divide and Conquer.'

'Divide and Rule,' I said.

'Divide and Conquer—Julius Caesar.'

'Divide and Rule,' I said, 'Matthew twelve, verse twenty-five.'

'Bullshit.'

'True,' I said. 'You don't believe me, check it out.'

'He is right, you know,' Ursula said.

None of this chat was of any consequence except to some infernal machine which might, just might, be relaying it. We could not possibly know whether or not the Cousins had spent enough time in the flat to implant one of these devices.

'Anyway, who cares?' Charlie said. 'It's time for beddie-byes. Farrow—'

'You don't have to tell me,' I said. 'I'll go and clean my teeth before you monopolise the plumbing.'

'After you,' Ursula said.

'Right then, Farrow, on your way.'

After brushing my teeth, I made going-to-bed noises. Modern surveillance gear can pick up the sound of a very thin mouse as it sneaks across a very thick rug. When the walls began to reverberate to a rushing of water in the bath I hurried, stocking-footed, into the bathroom. He was perched on the edge of the tub, with Ursula perched beside him. He motioned us to keep our heads close together and, 'Ursula,' he breathed, 'get to a phone—not here in the flat—and tell your boss I want this place swept. I want it swept *now*, immediately.'

'Difficult,' Ursula said.

'I don't want to know about "difficult", and tell him I said

34

so.'

'I will.'

'And go out quietly. Don't bang any doors.'

Ursula touched his arm, and smiled a smile that was almost coquettish. 'It will be quite easy,' she said, 'I have a very good friend who lives just across the hall, and we have keys to each other's flats. I do not need to leave the building.'

Charlie took her on trust. Me, I wondered who the *very good* friend was.

'Okay, off you go,' Charlie said. We listened for any sounds of her leaving. There were none. 'Right, then,' Charlie went on, 'get into bed and start snoring.'

'And you splash about,' I said.

\*　　　\*　　　\*

Willy was good. He was very good. He arrived within the hour, and he came alone with his gadgets concealed in the pockets of his overcoat. In the meantime we'd made all the normal noises. We heard his car draw up, and we heard his pseudo-drunken calls towards the window of the flat above from which dying sounds of revelry still emanated. We heard him clump up the stairs, but we did not hear him creep back down to enter our open front door.

Charlie, smelling of soap and bath-salts, in pyjamas and dressing gown. Me wearing shirt and trousers, no shoes. Ursula still fully dressed, which made me somewhat disappointed. What an attractive kid. She caused me to wish I was twenty years younger. None of us spoke a word until Willy had finally done his stuff with those marvellous electronic toys which still remain a mystery to me. When he finally pocketed a pocket-size scanner and shed his overcoat, it fell with a thud where he dropped it.

'Nothing.'

'You sure?' Charlie said.

'I tell you, nothing. They could not have had time.'

'You'd better be damned sure,' Charlie said.

'Hey, come on, mate.'

'You shut up.'

35

'Jesus, Charlie!' I said.

'Go and get your head down.'

'Bollocks!'

'A small cognac,' Schumacher said. He addressed himself to Ursula, who went off to get it.

'So you're positive?' Charlie said.

'Yes, I am positive, I am absolutely positive. They might have people outside, but I do not think so. I checked most carefully.'

'Most carefully,' Charlie said. He said it as though he doubted it.

'Your cognac,' Ursula said. Schumacher took it and tossed it back and handed her the empty glass and his body signals, loud and clear, said he wouldn't mind another one. Ursula nodded, and turned away. 'I will fill it up,' she said.

'No, you won't. He's driving, and we've all got to get to bed.'

'Relax, old buddy.'

'When I want your advice . . .'

'All right, knackers,' I said.

'I will see you out,' said Ursula.

'Not necessary,' Schumacher said. He hefted his overcoat up off the floor, laboriously shrugged it on, and nodded at Charlie. 'Take care, my friend.'

'Likewise,' Charlie said, 'and don't forget what I told you earlier.'

'How could I?' Schumacher said. He flashed me a glance which spoke volumes, nodded at Ursula, and was out and away in a matter of seconds.

'You should have thanked him, Charlie,' I said.

'Don't you tell me what I should have done.'

'I'm telling you,' I said, 'you should have kept him sweet. You've offended him.'

'Good. Keeps him on his toes.'

'One of these days, you're going to get us both killed.'

'If that's what you think,' he said, 'you ought to increase your insurance cover.' He was reaming fingernails already as clean as my granny's used to be before she kneaded the dough for our bread. He looked up through shiny rimless spectacles, stowed the nail file away, smoothed his damp hair, and almost smiled. 'You'd better get some kip. We've an early start in the morning.'

'If I'm asleep, don't wake me,' I said.

Ursula was sitting in the kitchen, waiting for us to retire before she made a last visit to the bathroom. I sat down opposite, and we looked at each other across the plastic-topped table. I reached out to cover her hand. It felt small and soft and awfully vulnerable. She wrinkled her nose in a grin which roiled my senses with turbulent emotions; remembrances of myself when young, and a consequent stirring of dormant lusts. She obviously inferred my distress, because she latticed our fingers and squeezed very gently. Guilt made me lower my eyes, and withdraw my hand.

'It's all right,' she said quietly.

'Listen, luv,' I said, 'you don't have to get mixed up in this business.'

'But I choose to. It is as your friend said. I am all grown up, and I have a mind of my own.'

'Yes, I know,' I said, 'but I want you to change it. Give up, and get out.'

Smiling, she shook her head, and leaned across the table to touch my lips.

'Go to bed, and rest,' she said.

\*       \*       \*

The going to bed was relatively easy, but to rest was something else. My sleep was plagued by spasmodic dreams which, on waking, seemed bizarre. Distorted fragments of real incidents long past ludicrously brought up to date and related to the imminent future. Freud would have had a ball. I was tantalised by images of Ursula which, when I reached out to hold, metamorphosed into images of Charlie and Willy Schumacher and various of the Others who were long since dead. I woke, and tossed and turned, but Charlie slept like a baby.

37

# THURSDAY

'Rise and shine,' he said. 'Come on, Farrow, rise and shine.'

He was nudging me with his foot. When I groaned and rolled over, the sleeping bag rolled with me. I was stiff from lying on the floor, and my poorly leg was aching.

'All right, all right!' I said.

'Never mind "all right", it's after seven.'

I un-gummed one bleary eye, and looked at my watch. It was five minutes past. I knew without looking up that he'd be laved and shaved and dressed in a brushed blue suit and a fresh white shirt and, doubtless, clean underwear. I struggled up out of the sleeping bag and sat on the edge of the bed, yawning and scratching my scrotum.

'For Christ's sake,' Charlie said, 'cover yourself up. Get some clothes on.'

'And you get knotted,' I said.

But I staggered into the bathroom, which was full of scented steam, and wiped off the fog which obscured the mirror. The face which looked back at me was a travesty of the one I'd always lived with. 'This isn't you,' I said, 'this is the picture you keep in the attic.'

'You talking to me?' Charlie said.

'No, I'm not. I'm talking to me.'

'Stop arseing around, then,' he said.

I scraped the stubble off my cheeks, and washed my hair in the bath, and then felt better. But not a lot. The morning did not bode well. No salivating aroma of crisping bacon, no sizzling of eggs in the pan, just the omnipresent odour of coffee. Small wonder the Germans lost the war. Any nation content to start the day on a breakfast of bread and jam fully deserves its come-uppance.

'*Guten Morgen*,' Ursula said. 'Did you sleep well?'

'Oh, sure,' I said, 'you've got the softest concrete floor in Kronberg.'

'I'm sorry about that,' she said. 'I had thought you might have shared the bed.'

'We're not such close friends,' I said.

38

'Would you like some coffee?'

'I'd rather have tea.'

'Milk and sugar?'

'Yes, please.'

'I'm afraid the rolls are not very fresh.'

'Doesn't make much difference,' I said.

*'Bitte?'* Her frown was so ingenuous, it made me feel like a heel.

'Oh, nothing,' I said, 'it was just a joke.'

'I could give you some strawberry jam . . .'

'That's grand,' I said, 'that would be lovely.'

She was wearing a long dressing gown over a slightly longer nightie, and slippers. The old Adam stirred in my loins. She smelled very subtly but unmistakably of very clean and healthy young girl. I tried to concentrate on the buttering of my roll.

'There you are . . .' she said, 'one cup of tea, and one pot of jam.'

'Lovely, smashing,' I said.

'Now if you'll excuse me, I'll go and dress.'

'Take your time,' I said.

'What the hell did you mean, "take your time"?' said Charlie.

'Ah, the wanderer's return. Finished your packing, have you?'

'Is that a fresh pot of tea?'

'I thought you'd had yours?'

'Don't get snotty.'

'What—on bread and jam? I only get snotty on ham and eggs.'

'Get it down you. There isn't much time.'

'When is there ever?'

'I said, don't get snotty!'

I took a long gulp of weak tea, and began to butter my second roll. 'All right, but now tell me,' I said, 'exactly how the Cousins got onto us last night, and what the hell took them so long.'

'Simple. Routine airport surveillance. We were recognised coming in.'

Well, nothing really incredible about that. We were not

exactly unknown, and in each other's company might hardly be missed.

'Okay, so they spotted us, and they spotted Ursula.'

'Gets you ten out of ten.'

'But I thought we made sure we weren't followed?'

'Beyond the city limits, yes. But do you think they don't know Willy's people, that they don't know where Ursula lives?'

'So as soon as we took the turn-off for Kronberg, the rest was A,B,C. And you suspected as much, you devious bastard.'

'Sticks and stones,' he said.

'So why the hell didn't you say so?'

'You didn't need to know.'

'Maybe. But now, I *do* need to know.'

'Need to know what?' he said, and with such bland surprise I almost believed it.

'Westerholme,' I said, 'what took him so long to get here?'

'Jesus, Farrow,' he said. 'He had to be fetched from wherever he was, because the local boys needed him to make a positive identification. He's the only one they've got who actually knows us.'

'Thank you.'

'Thank me for what?'

'For admitting to something I already knew.'

'If you knew, why ask?' he said. Then, 'Listen, get your finger out!'

'Not so fast,' I said. I brushed dry crumbs off my fingers and topped up my cup of tea, and wiped my mouth on the back of my hand. 'There's one thing more.'

'Like what?'

'Like to what extent must we use Willy's people?'

'Keep your voice down!' he hissed.

I shot a glance towards the bathroom. The door was firmly closed, and I closed my mind to what lay beyond. But:

'I'm telling you, Charlie,' I said, 'I want that girl left out of it.'

'Tell Schumacher, he's her boss.'

'So Willy's in charge, then?'

40

'Like hell he's in charge!'

'Exactly, and that's what I mean.'

We were interrupted by Ursula, all rosy from her bath. 'If you're finished in the bedroom, I'll go and dress.'

'You do that,' Charlie said.

When she had closed the door behind her, 'And there's something else,' I said.

'No, there isn't. I've had enough of your whingeing.'

'Listen—'

'I said, that's enough!'

So I abandoned my quest for knowledge, drank what was left of the tea, and went off to answer a call of nature. As I was washing my hands, Charlie knocked on the bathroom door.

'Come on, Farrow, shake it up!' They both had their coats on, ready for the off, and our luggage was out in the hall. 'Ursula, go and get the car. Farrow, you bring the bags.'

We were swiftly embroiled in the rush-hour traffic, and our drive to the airport was grim. I thought such slow progress might have set Charlie fuming, but he seemed uncharacteristically relaxed. When Ursula dropped us off at Departures she immediately drove away, and I said to Charlie:

'What's all this, then?'

'Just grab the gear,' he said.

He limped on ahead, and I hefted the cases, and it wasn't until we checked in that I knew we were booked on a domestic to Munich. I sighed, and tagged along. Once upstairs in the waiting area Charlie fished out a paperback book and settled down to a quiet read. I just gazed around, and wondered what the hell was going on. When our flight was called, Charlie nudged me and murmured, 'Hang on.'

We let the eager beavers surge forward in their mad rush to claim reserved seats, and attached ourselves to the end of the queue. Then Charlie, who always knew where everything was, including the packet of three which had lain for years behind bottles of old medicines in *my* bathroom cabinet, couldn't find his boarding pass.

'I must have it somewhere,' he said.

'Try your inside pocket.'

41

'I've tried it, for Christ's sake!' he said, but he tried it again. No boarding pass.

'All right, keep calm,' I said. Laurence Olivier, pack your bags, and I didn't know what sort of part he assumed I knew I was acting. 'You got it when we checked in, and we came straight up here.'

'I know!'

'So *think*, then. What did you do with it?'

'Look, if I knew that,' he said, 'I wouldn't have lost it, would I?'

Everyone else was now gone, and the 'plane was waiting down there on the apron, and the lass on boarding-checks was showing signs of losing her patience.

'I am sorry, sir . . . ' she said.

Charlie smacked his forehead, 'Of course! I slipped it into my book!'

'Then where is your book, sir?'

On the seat, where he'd left it.

'Please hurry, then,' the girl said, and no prizes for guessing who it was did the hurrying. As we stepped out into the mobile gantry she shut the door with a bang, and I imagined her thinking *bloody foreigners*! and justifiably, too.

The movable tunnel was deserted until we turned around its bend. Then, as we veered at an angle towards the aircraft's hatch, we were met by a small reception committee. The still-open hatch was unmanned, and I could hear a faint crackle of radio traffic as the pilot ran through his checks.

'Well done, Willy,' Charlie said.

Schumacher indicated his two companions. 'This is Kurt Schmidt, and this—'

'Never mind,' Charlie said, 'but I want my suitcase on the next flight back.'

Never a word about mine.

'Yes, of course. It is all arranged.'

So the pieces fell into place, and the jigsaw became much less of a puzzle. The man whose name was Kurt Schmidt wore rimless glasses and a dark blue raincoat and was Charlie's height and build and his hair—a wig?—looked remarkably similar. He wasn't an identical twin, but he was close enough to fool any spotter in Munich working from a photograph. Likewise my own nameless 'double'.

'Right, then,' Charlie said, 'they'd better get on board—but what about *him*?'

He nodded towards a fourth man who was standing at the gantry controls, wearing the uniform of an airport worker.

'One of ours,' Willy said. 'Don't worry, he will keep his mouth shut.'

'He bloodywell better,' Charlie said.

'Jesus, Charlie!'

'You shut up,' he prodded Kurt Schmidt in the chest to punctuate his next remark, 'and you, Herr Schmidt,' he went on, '*don't* forget the limp—okay?'

'He will not forget,' Willy said.

When our *alter egos* had boarded the plane, but before the hatch had been closed, I said, 'What now?'

'We wait,' said Willy.

'That's right. We wait,' Charlie said.

'Wait for what?'

'Don't pee yourself.'

But the confines of that claustrophobic tunnel were closing in on me, and I could feel the sweat trickling down my ribs. One very good reason why I had never volunteered for submarine service. I could never abide being hemmed in. The following few minutes seemed like hours, but there soon came the welcome sound of a hissing of hydraulics and then a muted *clunk* as the aircraft hatch was made secure.

'Okay, that's it,' I said.

'Is it hell as like. For Christ's sake relax.'

And so I sweated it out until the telescopic gantry began to creep back on itself, like some gigantic concertina. By which time the plane was away, taxiing towards the perimeter track, and I saw no reason at all why we shouldn't escape from that awful cocoon.

'Let's get out of this thing,' I said.

Charlie's glare would have frozen Hell's fires.

'Soon, but not yet,' Willy said.

We had to stay hidden until the flight was airborne. I was forced to suffer my fears until the Cousins' watchers were satisfied that all who had boarded the 'plane were up and away and committed to Munich. Establish a firm precedent, and that which follows is taken for granted. Spotters at the other end would see what they expected to see, and contact Westerholme, and then he would take a following flight. That was when I knew that whatever was going to happen had to happen soon, before Westerholme realised that Charlie had tricked him.

As though he had read my thoughts, Schumacher said, 'Charles, Kurt Schmidt is *good*. He will keep them occupied until we are finished here in Frankfurt.'

'Let's just hope you're right,' Charlie said. 'Now, I trust you've arranged a way out of here?'

'Come on, let's *go*!' I said.

\* \* \*

In airports, the flow of human traffic is directed along certain ways by signs accepted as being imperative. But they don't know the half of it. There are many doors which are always kept locked, opened only by special keys, and others disguised as shelves stacked high with displays of perfumes or booze. There is nothing sinister about these measures, they are there to guard and protect the innocent traveller against terrorism.

But they have other uses, too. We were able to leave the airport complex via doors and corridors forbidden to the general public, and we finally emerged after tramping what seemed to me like miles, into blessed open air. We stepped out onto a secluded apron way out in the freight area to find a car waiting there for us. I recognised it at once. It was the very same BMW which Charlie and I had used after stealing it from Willy on the Leipzig job. I'm sure that Charlie knew, but after we'd settled ourselves in the back:

'Nice car, Willy,' he said. 'Is it your own, or is it the firm's?'

'Just ignore him,' I said.

Willy looked up into the mirror as he negotiated a turn which revealed a high security gate. '*Ja, Ich verstehe*,' he said.

Charlie said, 'Speak English!'

44

'Sod off, Charlie,' I said, 'you speak better German than both of us put together.'

'You watch yourself,' Charlie said.

At the time, I felt pissed off with him, but looking back over the years, I perceive the extent of his dedication. Me, I did each job to the best of my abilities: him, he gave his whole life. He never relaxed or doubted or wavered, and he never questioned himself because he knew *precisely* who he was and *why* he was doing what he did.

We reached the safe house in bright winter sunshine which made me feel naked, and exposed, but I drew some comfort from the fact that Charlie seemed quite at ease. And the exposure lasted only a very few seconds. As we stepped onto the porch, Ursula opened wide the front door and stood back to let us nip inside. When she had closed the door behind us, 'How did it go?' she said.

Willy said, 'Fine, it went perfect.'

'Don't count your chickens,' Charlie said.

Ursula shot me a tiny grin. 'I will make us some coffee,' she said.

'You got any tea?'

'I think so.'

'Make mine tea, then,' Charlie said.

'Same for me, luv. Milk and sugar.'

'Yes, I remember,' she said.

Willy said, 'I will have coffee, and a brandy.'

'Listen,' Charlie said, as he took off and shook out his raincoat, 'what's all this boozing lark?'

'Hey, Chas, take it easy.'

'You, belt up.'

'Relax, Charles,' Willy said. 'An occasional brandy never hurt anyone.'

'Occasional, hell!' Charlie said. 'I noticed you were at it last night, and now you're at it again, and it's only eleven o'clock in the morning.'

'Don't concern yourself,' Willy said.

'You bet your bloody life I concern myself. This isn't a picnic we're on.'

'Let us go into the sitting-room.'

'After you, Charlie,' I said.

When we were seated in that dreary room, 'I'm sorry . . .' Willy said.

'Don't be sorry. Just stay sober.'

'It's one small brandy, Charles.'

'One dose of that poison leads to another. After tonight, you can sup yourself silly, but until we're all free and clear, I want you fully *compos mentis*.'

'You are making too much of this thing.'

'He's right, Chas,' I said. 'Christ, leave it alone.'

'You mind your own business,' he said.

I was still trying to think up a cutting reply when Ursula returned with the drinks. Four steaming mugs, and a lone glass of brandy. Willy Schumacher eyed the glass as she stooped to set down the tray, and I suddenly began to share Charlie's concern. Willy was having trouble with his lips, and I knew the feeling only too well. It happens to most of us, and as we grow older in the Business, the occasions multiply. It has to do with the ageing process. Youth is a prop of itself, but youth is sadly ephemeral, and nerves stretched too often become less elastic.

'Sit yourself down, luv,' I said.

Charlie was looking at Willy, who was looking at the brandy glass. I lifted my mug of sad weak tea, and 'Beautiful. Cheers,' I said.

Ursula and I exchanged covert glances. We were just pawns in this game. Willy's hand passed over the brandy to reach for his coffee mug, and as he lifted it up to his lips:

'That's the way, Willy. Cheers,' Charlie said.

Willy left the liquor untouched, and my heart went out to him. I knew the effort it must have cost and I knew that, in no small way, we might be responsible for his present condition. Our success on the Leipzig job had made him appear incompetent towards the end of a fine career, and such humiliation is not easy to live with.

So, '*Gesundheit*, Willy,' I said. 'Sup up, and sup your brandy.'

'Thank you, Farrow.'

'Be my guest.'

I didn't turn my head to look at Charlie. I could *feel* his furious glare, but Ursula had chosen to sit beside me on the sofa, and her thigh was alongside mine, and I imagined a slight but definite pressure.

'All right then,' Charlie said, 'when you've all stopped licking each other's arses—'

'Hey! Steady on!' I said.

'—we might get down to business.'

'Yes, of course,' Willy said. He had still not yet touched the brandy, and I admired his self-control. It could not have been easy. I had seen all the signs. 'Where do you wish to begin?'

Charlie began by composing himself. Not in the abstract sense, because the bugger was always mentally composed at any time of day or night and whatever the prevailing circumstance. His actions were designed to *dis*compose all present company. I watched him, yet again, perform the old familiar routine. First, the shiny rimless spectacles carefully unhooked and polished on one of his spotless white handkerchiefs. Same hankie to ream out his nose, and finally to flick imaginary dust off his gleaming black lace-up shoes before being consigned to obsolescence. Then, a settling of his attire. A hand-brushing down of his jacket and waistcoat, a check on the knot of his tie, and alignment of his trousers' creases dead-centre over his knees. But with Ursula's young shank warm against mine, I was blissfully unimpressed.

'Are you ready now, Charlie?'

'You, shut your gob.'

'Very well,' Schumacher said. He paused to sip coffee. Only coffee. 'So far as I can see, there should be no problem. No problem at all.'

'Is that a fact?' Charlie said.

'We have a plan of the barracks.'

'Let's see it, then,' Charlie said.

'Ursula?'

'Yes, I will get it.'

When she rose and left the room, she seemed to take all of the warmth of it with her. In the brief hiatus which followed:

'Can I ask a question?' I said.

'No,' Charlie said. 'Just shut up, and listen.'

47

'Charles. Charles—*please* . . .' Willy said.

Ursula returned with a plan of the barracks. Charlie took it from her, and studied it for the space of several seconds before glancing up at her.

'Is this the only copy?'

'It is.'

'You *sure*?'

'Yes.'

'Good,' Charlie said, and began to tear it into small pieces.

'Wait!'

'It's all right, Willy,' I said. The plan would be etched on the photographic plate which Charlie used for a brain.

With the sheet of paper reduced to confetti, Charlie said, 'Where's the loo?'

'Give it to Ursula. She will do it.'

'I'll do it myself,' Charlie said.

'There is a toilet at the end of the hall.'

When we heard the distant flushing of a lavatory, '*Scheisse!*' Willy Schumacher said, 'your friend trusts nobody!'

'You better believe it. Not even his mother,' I said. 'Assuming, of course, that he ever had one.'

'I like him,' Ursula said. 'He is just a big rough teddy-bear.'

'Bears have claws,' Willy said.

'You never spoke a truer word.'

'Yes, and you too,' he said. Then, to Ursula, 'This one also has claws.'

Was he hinting, or what? Was he nursing a yen for Ursula? Was it vulgar jealousy, or was he just being protective, caring for one of his own? Whatever his motive, I felt curiously flattered. No fool like an old fool.

'Leave off! I'm only a common labourer.'

'Oh, yes, we know,' Willy said.

'Willy—*please!*' So she called him 'Willy'.

'Look, let's forget it,' I said.

I had heard a second flushing of the lavatory, and Willy had heard it too. He sank his brandy in one large gulp and signalled, as it went down, for Ursula to remove all the

48

empties. The lass responded fast, but not quite fast enough to beat Charlie. As she passed him with her tray, I saw that he noted the empty glass.

'Feeling better now, Willy?' he said.

'McGowan, this is ridiculous!'

'I'm glad you agree,' Charlie said. 'So now, if you're not too befuddled...'

'I have *told* you that all is arranged!'

'I know you've told me, but tell me again.' Charlie's manner was mild, as though he was checking a shopping list.

Willy heaved a sigh. 'The reception will open at seven o'clock...'

This was the stuff they'd gone over after Ursula and I were dismissed that previous evening in Kronberg, but all of it was new to me, and I wanted to know what was happening. So, 'Just a minute,' I said. 'What's this reception we're talking about?'

'What's the date?' Charlie said. He sounded tired.

'It's the 24th.'

'Last Thursday in November?'

'Well, there won't be another,' I said.

'So what happens on the last Thursday?'

I suddenly recalled an occasion in San Francisco when I was staying with friends over there.

'Oh, I get it! The Cousins have a piss-up.'

'He's got it,' Charlie said.

'Yes,' Willy said, 'they call it Thanksgiving.'

'Okay, don't tell me,' I said. 'There's gonna be a good time in the old town tonight?'

'Yes. A party at the barracks,' Willy said.

'Are we invited, then, Charlie?'

'Don't talk wet,' he said.

'How else are we going to get in there?'

'Wait and see,' Charlie said.

\*       \*       \*

I found out in that same afternoon. After Ursula had rustled up a not-bad lunch she drove Charlie and I to a meet, at an

49

unspecified venue on the far side of town, with a brace of *very* V.I.P.s. There were no introductions, no shaking of hands. Anonymity was the order of the day. Both were elderly, well over sixty. One was West German, a three-star general with more ribbons on his chest than ever graced that of Montgomery. The other one reminded me of that well-known British actor always at his best in the part of a plenipotentiary. He was almost a clone of the Man, socked hard and solid into the upper Establishment. I saw the light at once, because even a blind man couldn't have missed it.

The house was smaller than the Palace of Westminster, but it was set in a large estate and was obviously a private residence the occupants of which had put the place on loan for an hour or so. The worldwide Old Boy network is geo-political, and has been so for several hundreds of years. The Rothschilds financed both British and French throughout the Napoleonic wars, and some people in the U.S. of A. were accumulating profits from factories in the Saar throughout the Second World War. Rudolph Hess flew to Scotland during the height of that war to confer with his buddies over there, and the reason his chat came to naught was due to the fact that he acted on his own without first consulting the Boys.

You don't believe it? Believe it.

This is just to digress, but I pondered upon such historical diversions as I sat in that splendid room of a house belonging to very rich owners whose wealth manifested itself in the calculated opulence of its furnishings. Teutonically splendid, but vaguely oppressive. Me, I much preferred the honest simplicity of my old Yorkshire farmhouse.

Having delivered us to the meet, Ursula took herself off. Possibly into the nether regions, but maybe to sit in the car. The general had opened the door to us, and we never saw another soul between our arrival and departure. I wondered, as is my wont, where the hell all the servants were hiding. Which left just the four of us, with me feeling like the spare man at a wedding. Charlie, damaged as he was by injuries which might have killed lesser men, dominated the scene. The German general and the British diplomat waited impatiently until Charlie had completed his preliminary routine: the polishing of his spectacles, the arrangement of his attire, the reaming of his nose, and the check on his shoes. This was what made the Business so fascinating. The Man had passed the word, and the name of the word was Charles McGowan, and Charlie was a considerable man. He affected the role of obedient servant whilst contriving, all the while, to leave no doubt as to who was In Charge. I just sat there and listened.

After some preliminary sparring, the German soldier said, 'There is serious danger, here, of offending our American friends.'

Charlie passed that one to the elderly gentleman. A diplomatic cough deflected by a manicured hand, a smoothing of shining white hair, and a downwards glance at the old school tie. Blue, with a silver stripe. 'Yes,' he said, 'quite so.' He wasn't talking to the German general. 'You people must understand—'

'Oh, we *do* understand,' said Charlie, smooth-talking bugger that he was. 'Believe me, sir, we *do* understand.' His frown was like that of a vicar offended by the sight of a dirty mark on a choirboy's surplice.

It all seemed to me like a weird charade, though I knew too well it was *real*. What quickly emerged from the welter of double-talk was that Charlie and I were to accompany the diplomat to the Thanksgiving shindig as his minder and chauffeur, and guess who was to do the driving. The general's regular staff was to be replaced by Willy and Ursula, with the latter acting as chauffeuse. The bigwigs were patently unhappy with the arrangement, obviously unaware of the purpose behind the exercise. Neither of them asked any pertinent questions, I inferred they just didn't want to know.

So the meeting was short, if not sweet, and Charlie wound it up in his usual manner. 'That's it then, sir,' he said. 'Now, if we might have the I.D. papers . . .'

'I have them here,' the man said. He probed the inner pocket of his immaculate jacket and produced a stiff envelope. 'I hope you'll find everything in order.'

It was plain he hoped nothing of the kind. His attitude

51

suggested he was hoping that nothing was in order and that, somehow, he'd be let off the hook.

Charlie took the envelope, and, 'Thank you, sir,' he said. 'We'll join you at the consulate, as arranged.'

'Very well,' the man said. 'But I do hope you people know what you're doing.'

What he really meant was, 'You'd better not drop us in the shit.'

'Absolutely,' the general said.

Charlie said, 'Gentlemen, have no fears.' He paused at the door, and turned. 'I'm sure your co-operation will be properly appreciated.'

What *he* really meant was this: 'You remain paid-up members of the Old Boys' Club.'

Nobody said 'Goodbye'.

\*       \*       \*

As Ursula drove us away in the car, 'Jesus, Charlie,' I said, 'I never thought I'd see you lick *that* kind of bum.'

'Farrow, shut up,' he said.

He laid his head back against the squab and the lines of strain on his face seemed etched in black against the pallor of his skin.

'Are you all right?' I said.

'Of course I'm all right. What the hell are you getting at?'

'You're not all right,' I said.

'Shut up. Take a look at these, and tell me what you think.'

He fished the stiff envelope out of his pocket, and handed it over to me. Inside were two identity jotters, complete with photographs, in names which matched those on our funny passports. The seals and signatures appeared to be genuine, good Foreign Office stuff. I guessed that the Man was owed a lot of favours and that, now, he was calling them in.

'I'd say that these are the real McCoy.'

'They better be,' Charlie said.

He spoke with closed eyes, and his head still laid back, and I was seized by conflicting emotions. A nagging

52

premonition that the job was doomed to go wrong. Like, the last shall be first, and the first shall be last. Yet, and at the same time, I felt myself responsible. I felt that I had to Take Charge, and to stand at the epicentre was curiously invigorating. I had a vision of myself as McKenzie's saviour, and Champion of the Man. With Charlie, for once, relying on *me* instead of it being the reverse.

But the spasm of elation was fleeting, and before we were back at the house I had begun once again to worry about Charlie. He appeared to doze on the way, but I wouldn't have wanted to bet on it. He was probably making a sham in order to deter me from asking the questions which seethed around in my mind. Our basic *modus operandi* was, of course, perfectly clear. We were to infiltrate the U.S. barracks, take possession of Dorf, smuggle him out, and swap him for McKenzie. With impunity, that is, for the German general and our man in Frankfurt. This last posed a monumental snag. The getting-in would present no problem, but getting ourselves—and Dorf—out, with no possible compromise of the V.I.P.s, raised a tumult of doubt in my mind. All right, so Willy had assistance In Place, but what could Sergeant Kramer do whilst all the time desperate to cover his arse? I knew that Charlie had a scheme just as surely as I knew that, ask as I may, he would not reveal it to me on the perfectly reasonable grounds that the best-laid plans of mice and men . . . So he would carry the plan in his skull, and adapt it *in situ* second-by-second. He had that ability, and all I could do was to go along in a spirit of absolute trust, and rely on his instant judgement.

That my faith in him had been justified over more than twenty-five years is evidenced by our still being alive, and the telling of this tale. But the fears I felt that day in Frankfurt were of a different kind to any I had ever felt before, because these fears were not for myself. For the first time ever, my fears were for Charlie. He was drawing on reserves of strength beyond, it seemed, even *his* resources.

'Wakey, wakey,' I said.

He opened his eyes and was instantly alert. 'When you catch a weasel asleep—'

'I know,' I said, 'you piss in its ear.'

53

'Oh, you remembered,' he said.

Ursula had driven us back to her flat. Willy was waiting for us. So, too, were a pair of large guns. Laid out, in their holsters, on the coffee table.

'What's all this?' Charlie said.

'Special dispensation,' said Willy.

'Jesus!' Charlie said, and sank into a chair without taking off his raincoat. 'If you believe a shoot-out, Willy, you'll believe about anything.'

'Of course not,' Schumacher said, 'but—'

'But *nothing*! If it comes to fireworks, the whole bloody job's down the drain!'

I had picked up one of the pistols. Smith & Wesson .357. I slid it out of its holster, and checked the cylinder. Fully loaded, magnum rounds.

'Why not, Charlie?' I said. 'Better safe than sorry.'

'Jesus!' Charlie said. Then, 'Farrow, go talk to your girl friend.'

'But he's right,' Willy Schumacher said.

Only Charlie was sitting. He sighed, and looked up at us.

'When I say no guns, I mean no guns.'

'I'll see you boys later,' I said, and left the buggers to sort it out.

Ursula had gone straight to the kitchen. She wasn't doing anything, she was just back there, still with her coat on, her splendid little rump propped against one of the worktops.

'So what is going on?' she said.

'Good question,' I said. 'Don't you ever get the feeling that whatever's going on has little or nothing to do with *us*?'

'Let me give you some whisky,' she said. She opened a cupboard and let me see a bottle. 'Do you like it?'

'Beautiful,' I said, and I wasn't referring to the whisky. Some people have qualities which stir the heart, and the heart is stirred by emotions only some of which are inspired by sex.

'How long do you think they will continue to talk?' She was pouring a jar for me, and had paused with the neck of the bottle on the tumbler.

'I don't give a monkey's,' I said, 'and you can give me about the same again.'

That delightful bewitching grin, and she sloshed in a further full measure. 'Some water?'

'Yes, please,' I said.

'Mr McGowan will be angry with you.'

'Situation normal,' I said.

We pulled out chairs, and sat at the table, and she cupped her chin in her hands. 'But seriously, I am worried.'

'You and me both,' I said, 'which is why I want you out of it.'

'Why?'

'Because ... well, *because*,' I said.

'Because you knew my mother?'

'No. Because I know you,' I said.

She reached across the table, and patted the back of my hand. 'I have told you, I can take care of myself.'

'Christ! What's the use?' I said.

Such serenity of confidence is the prerogative of Youth, and however misplaced it remains essential to the future of all of us. A concept engendered by whisky fumes? I buried my nose in my glass, conscious much more of her presence than I was of the fire in my throat. The idyll was rudely interrupted. Story of my life. A voice at my back said:

'Finished, then, are you?'

'Just about,' I said.

Charlie was at the kitchen door, hands in raincoat pockets, eyes like water in a pond, with Willy Schumacher peering over his shoulder. Somewhat anxiously. Ursula had detected their approach way ahead of me, a matter of three or maybe four seconds. Whatever, my empty glass was now enfolded in both of her hands, and mine held nothing at all.

'Right, you two. Willy's leaving.'

'I hope it keeps fine for him, then.'

'Farrow, don't be a smart-arse.'

'Heavens forefend,' I said.

He smelled it on me. I knew he would. He could detect a brewer's dray at a distance of something like half a mile. Ursula had done her best, but nobody's best was enough to fool Charlie.

The lass was up on her feet, trying to pour oil on troubled

waters.

'I will see you out, Willy,' she said.

When they were gone, Charlie looked at me, and 'Jesus Christ!' he said.

'Charlie, relax. It's my opinion—'

'Your opinion,' he said, 'is worth less than a particle of pigeon shit!'

'All right then, knackers,' I said.

\*       \*       \*

We spent what remained of that afternoon each unto our own. Charlie retired to the bedroom. I heard him using the phone, and hoped that the silence which followed meant he was having a kip. Ursula messed about, weeding her window-boxes and watering her plants and attending to small household chores. I noticed she didn't use the vacuum cleaner, or make any other kind of noise which might have disturbed someone sleeping. Me, I just slumped on the couch, pretending to read Robert L. Duncan. I couldn't concentrate. I was exercised by dire premonitions. Sign of advancing age. I even began to worry about *having* premonitions.

Presently, we heard the sound which accompanies Charlie wherever he goes: the gushing of water in a bath. We had moved to the kitchen, where the lass was making coffee. I glanced at the clock on the wall. Quarter past five already.

'Your friend is having a bath.'

'My friend is always having a bath. I just hope your water's hot.'

'Oh yes, there is plenty.'

'Thank God for that.'

Ursula used the bathroom after Charlie was finished, and he appeared at the kitchen door in his Paisley-pattern Tootal dressing gown.

'Come on, shake yourself.'

'Why?' I said. 'Are we going somewhere special?'

'Just get a move on,' he said.

When it came to my turn to use the ablutions, the water

56

was barely lukewarm, so I settled for a lick and a promise.

'You haven't had a shave,' Charlie said.

'I had a shave this morning.'

'That was this morning,' he said.

'What is this,' I said, 'a fashion parade?'

'Scruffy bugger!' he said.

\*     \*     \*

As Ursula drove us into Frankfurt, 'Listen, Charlie,' I said, 'we should have taken those .357s.'

'Why? What for?' he said, 'You want to start a war with the U.S. Army?'

'No. But—'

'Jesus!' he said.

\*     \*     \*

That night, the U.S. Army base at Frankfurt wore an air of gaiety which the small band of demonstrators outside could do little or nothing to dampen. The rain took care of that, their sad wet placards part-obscured by umbrellas. The message, ages-old, was 'Yanks Go Home'. That manner of sentiment. As though, if the Yanks did go home, all the ills of Europe would miraculously disappear, with Fortress America just a distant outpost. It was only a token demonstration as demonstrations go, but it added to my apprehensions. With the sort of job now in hand, we could well do without all this extra rhubarb.

Strange how matters of small importance later loom large in the mind. It was the first time, ever, I had driven a Rolls-Royce—although 'driven' was hardly correct. All I did was sit there in majesty and the great car drove itself in almost-eerie silence requiring no more effort from me than occasional touches of the steering wheel. The experience was like that of a dream, but when we drew up to the barracks gate I was brought down to earth with a bump.

It was as though the guard detail had been hand-picked for their abilities to intimidate. Talk about American football, every man was as big as a house even without the

armoured bodywear. Their big Colt's sidearms looked like
toy pistols. The Yanks do not do things by halves. When
they throw a party they throw a party and no matter in what
foreign field, they make very damn sure that their guests
will enjoy it. Demonstrators Go Home. You are farting
against implacable thunder.

Just a suggestion of foot on brake and the Rolls-Royce
stopped of itself, the big flat bonnet just short of the
barricade. I couldn't find the proper switch, but it didn't
matter because Charlie was ahead of me. As his nearside
front window slid down, he presented our jotters for
scrutiny. The hard-faced M.P. who took them from him
said:

'Sir. One moment, sir.'

He held a flashlight on us, then turned it on the
documents, and an age seemed to pass before he handed
them back. Meantime, our man in the rear might have been
excused for wetting himself. He sat way back there in all of
his finery, isolated it seemed, and aloof from these petty
proceedings. My armpits had started to sweat, but Charlie
might have been attending some garden fête. He watched
the M.P. check his clipboard, a bored expression on his face.
Not a bored expression. An *absence* of expression. He never
spoke a word. And neither did I, because my mouth was too
dry. The demonstrators had set up a chant, which was
being ignored by all concerned. I was vaguely aware of it as
the soldier gave our jotters back to Charlie.

'Sir, go straight ahead—' he was stooping to point a
white-gloved finger '—an' make a left, then a right, an'
there'll be somebody tell you where to park it.' U.S. soldiers
are so polite, you almost *want* them to shoot you.

The entire façade of the officers' mess was strung with
coloured lights. Not very dignified, but definitely festive. I
tooled the Rolls alongside, and Charlie nipped out to open
the back door. I was conscious of our man alighting, but
only marginally. The forefront of my mind was occupied by
a roiling flood of relief at having gained safe ingress. The
egress was something else but, like Scarlett O'Hara, I
wouldn't think of that now. I would think about it later.

Charlie got back in the car and said, 'Right. Turn left, then right. Park it round the back.'

The 'back' was a large parade ground surrounded on all four sides by large slab-fronted barracks blocks, all of whose windows shed light. Christ, the whole damn place was aglow.

'Oh, this is just lovely,' I said.

'Stop shitting yourself, and get this thing parked.'

A white-helmeted M.P., white belt and white gaiters, was waving his white-gloved hands to beckon me on across the parade ground. We were far from his first customer. He had already marshalled two rows of large cars in straight lines back-to-back, and had started to form a third row.

'That's handy,' Charlie said.

So I guessed that wherever they were keeping Dorf was somewhere over on that side. It didn't do a lot towards cheering me up, but it was better than a kick in the groin. I parked the Rolls beside a black BMW and switched the engine off, then checked to see that I had switched it off properly because in that total absence of sound it was impossible to *hear* if the motor had stopped.

'What the hell are you doing?' Charlie said.

'Just admiring the cockpit layout. Listen, Chas—'

'Save it,' he said.

The pennant in front of the big Mercedes which was gliding up alongside was that of a high-ranking German officer. It had been a neat piece of work. I hadn't noticed them in the mirror, so they must have picked us up immediately before we turned into the barracks. Ursula, ten out of ten. A sideways glance confirmed that she was driving. Willy Schumacher was sitting beside her in the forward passenger seat. As I reached for the door handle, Charlie said:

'Wait.'

Another car drawing in, followed by yet another. The M.P. was waving his arms, slowing them down to get them parked properly.

'All right, *now*,' Charlie said, 'and forget the hugs and kisses.'

'I'm glad you reminded me,' I said.

I got out of the car, and stretched my arms. Stupid, when I

59

look back, because the driving seat of that beautiful Rolls was as comfortable as any armchair. Most of the drivers and minders had also quit their cars and were leaning against them, smoking and chatting. Willy got out of the Merc and, *'Guten Abend, Wie geht's?'* he said.

'Sorry, mate. I don't speak German.'

Willy looked at the Union Jack which, limp from the drizzle, drooped sadly on its standard on the bonnet of the Rolls.

'Ah,' he said, 'you are English.'

'Make that "British",' I said.

'Of course,' he said. *'Great* Britain.'

'You taking the piss out of me?'

*'Bitte?* What is "taking the piss"?'

'Never mind,' I said. 'Introduce me to your girl friend.'

'Girl friend?'

'All right, then, your driver,' I said. Other cars were coming in, and the M.P. was moving away to line them up with military precision. When I was sure he was out of earshot, 'What's the score, Willy?' I said.

'So far,' he murmured, 'it is all quite perfect.'

'I'll tell the boss-man,' I said.

When I eased back into the Rolls, Charlie was doing his nails. He pressed down a wayward cuticle, held it up to the light, then went to work on another one. 'Well?'

'So far, so good,' I said.

My answer seemed to satisfy him. He continued his manicure, all the while humming a tuneless dirge. When at last he had finished, and had stowed his nail file away, I ventured a cheeky query.

'So what happens now?' I said.

By which time many more cars had rolled up, and the parade ground was almost half full, but new arrivals were becoming spasmodic.

'We sit here and wait,' Charlie said.

'Jesus Christ! How much longer?'

'Patience.'

'Patience, my arse!' I said.

My awareness of movement around the parade ground had been by peripheral sight, because the car's interior was quiet as the grave. But there had been considerable activity, a traffic of to-and-fro. Nothing from the car next to ours. Willy and Ursula still sat inside, as I could see by half-turning my head. Charlie affected to take no notice. Time dragged wearily. I looked again at the clock on the dashboard. I would have welcomed a measured beat, but the bloody thing was perfectly silent. No steady comforting tick, no yardstick by which to measure the minutes, so that every time I checked no more than two or three had passed.

The drizzle had finally stopped. No more specks on the windscreen. I let my window down, not so much for fresh air as for sensory perception. I wanted to hear something other than the sounds of our breathing. More than half an hour had passed since the trauma of getting into the barracks and the tension, having subsided, was beginning to rise again. Willy and Ursula had moved from the front to the rear of the Mercedes and were sitting at their ease in the back. Others of the drivers and minders were standing around in groups, smoking and talking. Waiting.

Waiting. It was getting on my tits.

I said, 'It's stopped raining.'

'Very observant.'

'Why don't we stretch our legs?'

'Why don't you shut your cake-hole?'

'Something's happening,' I said.

The M.P. sergeant who had marshalled the cars was moving from group to group, pausing at each to deliver a message. Charlie opened his eyes, and watched as the soldier drew closer. When he reached the Rolls, Charlie lowered the nearside window. The sergeant put both hands on the sill, and stooped almost double to peer in at us.

'Hey, you guys! Howya doin'?'

'Not so bad. How's yourself?' Charlie said.

'You wanna come over to the sergeants' mess, have yoreselves a snort?'

'Very kind, but we're not allowed.'

'Shit, man! Who's to know? The brass will be whoopin' it up fer hours!'

"We-e-ll . . . I'm not sure . . .' Charlie said.

'Like why should the brass have all the fun?'

'It's against the rules,' Charlie said.

Charlie appeared to think, but I knew damn well he had made up his mind. What I didn't know, and what I was not prepared for, was the *way* he had made it up.

'All right, then,' he said, 'we'll come one at a time.'

'Great!' the sergeant said. 'Stick around while I ask these others, an' we'll mosey on over—okay?'

When he turned away to the Mercedes, 'Windows,' Charlie said. I activated the windows, and when we were cocooned, 'Listen buggerlugs, one whiff of booze—'

'What's the point, then?' I said.

'Never you mind what the point is, be back here at ten to nine. That's ten to nine *exactly*—got it?'

'Yes, but—'

'No "buts",' he said. 'Keep off the poison. Drink lemonade.'

'Be bloody Coca Cola,' I said.

'I don't give a monkey's. Just remember.'

With that, he hopped out of the car and I saw him make signs to Willy from behind the sergeant's back. He was pointing at Ursula, and nodding. I couldn't hear what was being said, but that which ensued made it obvious. Ursula got out of the car, and let the sergeant take her arm. As the pair of them moved away, Charlie motioned for me to join them. I didn't know what was going on, I simply responded like one of Pavlov's dogs. The sergeant's attention was focused on Ursula, the only female in sight. As I hurried to catch up with them, someone called from behind.

'*Ursula—ein Moment, bitte!*'

All three of us turned around. Willy and Charlie were standing by the Merc. Willy beckoned Ursula back, leaving me with the sergeant.

'Shee-yit! What gives?' he said.

About half of the drivers and minders were converging from around and about, eager to get at the action.

'Don't ask me, sarge,' I said. 'Perhaps he's having second thoughts.'

'D'you reckon he wants to come first?'

'Well, one of 'em has to stay on the job.'

'Rather him, than her. He looks like a miserable

62

sonofabitch.'

'I wouldn't know,' I said, 'but she's certainly better-looking.'

'She sure is. She's a lulu.'

'Yes, I've noticed,' I said.

'You know her?'

'No. Never seen her before.'

'I wouldn't mind a piece of it.'

'So ask for her number.'

'I *got* her number.'

'I mean her telephone number,' I said. 'Who knows? She might be a right little raver.'

'I should be so lucky,' he said. 'These German ladies are kinda stand-offish.'

'So try a little harder,' I said.

'Oh, sure, but I got a wife on the base.'

'If you let that stop you,' I said, 'you'll never get anywhere, will you?'

'Why the hell are they takin' so long?' We were watching Willy and Ursula and Charlie, over by the cars. 'Your buddy seems to be doin' all the talkin'.'

'It's just his way,' I said. 'He was vaccinated with a gramophone needle.'

'Goes by the book, uh?'

'That's right.'

'I hope he's not gonna louse things up.'

'It's down to the Kraut,' I said.

I was making conversation in order to give Charlie time. Time to explain whatever plot had suddenly hatched in his mind. As I began to wax anxious that the thing was taking too long, that we might be arousing the sergeant's suspicions, Ursula turned away and tripped hurriedly towards us. The sergeant shot me a grin.

'I'd say she finally got clearance.'

'Looks that way,' I said.

When Ursula rejoined us, she took the sergeant's arm and flashed him a smile which looked perfectly genuine. 'So! It's arranged,' she said. 'I can stay until it's time for us to go.'

'Good for you,' I said.

We set off across the parade ground towards faint sounds

of revelry coming from a building on the opposite side.

'No, good for *you*,' she said. 'Your boss talked to my boss, and persuaded him to agree.'

The sergeant said, 'Hey! You talk good American!'

'She speaks good English,' I said.

'English, American—who the hell cares?'

'That's a bloody good question,' I said.

He laughed, and mock-punched me on the arm. The bugger didn't know his own strength. I knew he was only trying to be friendly but with his arm around Ursula's waist and his mind full of evil intentions, I hated the amiable sod. The three of us led an entourage heading for the sergeants' mess, the others following close on our heels, nattering amongst themselves. I knew that Ursula was acting a part, and I knew that I shouldn't mind, but I couldn't help minding. I *minded*.

'Well, folks, here we are!' The sergeant doffed his white helmet as he opened the big front door, throwing it wide and waving us all in. 'C'mon guys, hit the scene. Dump yore coats, an' get in there!'

Military barracks share a common design whosoever, and wherever, they are. Which seems odd to me, because every ship—even those of the same size and type—has a definite character all of its own. That U.S. Army mess in Frankfurt remains most memorable, though. Nothing to do with the fixtures and fittings, just a large rectangular room with a very long bar and lots of tables ranged around a small dance-floor. Music provided by a disco set-up. The noise, like the atmosphere, was intense. Several hundreds of people shouting to make themselves heard above the raucous 'music'. An air of jollity so thick you could carve it into slabs and stack it against the walls. The contagious excitement of a happy gathering crowd intent on enjoying itself. Some in uniform with ties dragged askew, others in off-duty gear perhaps better suited to a beach in Hawaii. A smattering of Army wives, most of them pretty and all of them shrill. The muzak, loud as it was, almost drowned by the din of chat and laughter. The overriding odour of food was evidenced by a draped buffet table stretching all along the back of the room, already much depleted.

64

Thanksgiving. Usually celebrated by family gatherings, in the privacy of their own homes. Anniversary of those first Thanks offered by the Pilgrim Fathers when they founded them U.S. of A. in the Year of Our Lord 1620. I wondered, as I looked around, how many of the revellers in this big 'family' actually appreciated what it was that the revels were all about. Not that it mattered, of course. Consider the vulgarity which passes for Christmas.

I felt a heavy hand on my elbow. 'You mind if I take her away?'

The sergeant, *sans* helmet, but not *sans* pistol. Bloody great Colt's .45. Left hand *almost* cupping a plump buttock, right hand shaking my arm. Ursula permitting the familiarity, ogling him like some little tart. Doubtless following instructions.

'Mind? Me? No,' I said. 'Why should *I* mind? Enjoy yourselves.'

'Jesus, you ain't got a drink! Whassamatter wit' you, ole buddy? Belly-up, now! What'll you have?' He pulled us both, me and Ursula, over to the bar, and shouted at one of the sweating orderlies. 'Hey, Kovacks! Get over here!'

I thought no less of Kovacks for rushing to obey the command. Private Soldier Kovacks was a worried-looking little G.I., and the sergeant was what they call a 'top-kick', and a big hard-faced bastard to boot.

'Yes, sarge?'

'Let's have some drinks here.' He turned to Ursula. 'Awright, honey, what'll it be?'

'Brandy and ginger ale, please. A small one. I have to drive.'

'An' I'll take a beer. You got that?'

Kovacks nodded, and looked up at me. 'Sir? What's your pleasure?' he said.

'Shooting and fishing and reading and music—'

'He is joking!' Ursula said.

'—and ale, and women. Not always in that order.'

The sergeant laughed, and punched me in the ribs. 'Jesus! You limeys!' he said. Then, to Ursula: 'C'mon, kid, let's mingle.'

Which left only Kovacks and me. Kovacks was anxious to

65

do his duty. 'Sir, what will you have?' he said.

'You got any Scotch?' To hell with Charlie.

'Sure. We got Ballantine's, an' Johnny Walker, an' Cutty Sark, an'—'

'Make it Ballantine's,' I said, 'equal amount of water.'

'Water?'

'As in faucet,' I said.

My watch said twenty-one minutes past eight. Half an hour to go, and I had to merge or else stand aloof, conspicuous to one and all. I don't know how many tables I sat at, or how much I pretended to drink. Americans are enormously generous people, and their hospitality is not easily declined. A sergeant and his wife from San Diego invited me to visit their home, and I do believe they were utterly sincere. As was the corporal from Boston, and the couple from New Mexico, and the lady from Seattle whose errant husband was dancing with another man's wife. Had the circumstances been different, I could have enjoyed myself. I could have free-loaded on Ballantine's whisky until the stuff ran out of my ears, and the potted plants in that sergeants' mess must even now stink of the stuff. When I think of all that good liquor I wasted . . .

I looked yet again at my watch. A quarter to nine, and the Thanksgiving party was getting into its stride. Hot and noisy and boisterous. I was sweating from the heat generated by hundreds of animated bodies. Ursula was nowhere to be seen. I hoped she was somewhere in the throng, and not whisked away by that big randy sergeant to some creaking army cot.

Simulating a drunken slur, 'I gotta go,' I said.

The wife from Seattle grabbed my arm. 'Aw, relax,' she said, 'the party ain't even started yet!'

'I'm supposed to be on duty,' I said. 'I'm prob'ly in trouble already.'

'Awright, so wait!' she said. She delved into her purse for a scrap of paper on which to scrawl a number. 'Call me.'

'I will,' I lied.

'You promise?'

'I promise.'

'It's best in the mornings.'

I still remember that lass. Mature, and buxom, but very attractive. Mamie. Ridiculous name, and strange that I should remember it now, but the whole is composed of its parts and one recollection prompts others.

The young G.I. on duty in the lobby tried to hide his beer. I affected not to notice, and as I put my raincoat on, I said: 'Hey, soldier, do you have any gum?'

'Sure. Be my guest,' he said. He gave me two strips of Wrigley's Spearmint. I peeled the wrappings off, and chewed the gum as I crossed the parade ground. The time was twelve minutes to nine. I reached the Rolls at ten-to precisely.

'About bloody time!' Charlie said.

I exuded a gust of Spearmint breath. 'You told me ten-to,' I said, 'and ten-to it is.'

'You been drinking?'

'For Christ's sake, Charlie!' I said.

'Right, then. Where's that sergeant?'

'So far as I know,' I said, 'he's heavily engaged with Ursula.'

'Let's bloodywell hope so,' he said.

While we were talking, Willy had joined us. 'I think we should go,' he said.

It had started to rain again, and the drivers and minders not at the party had ducked back into their cars. Charlie glanced all around and about, then, 'Right. Let's get on with it,' he said.

As he led us off at a strolling pace, cold fingers crawled up my spine. But the brighter the lights, the deeper the shadows, and we took advantage of them. The living quarters were probably deserted on this big party night, but we skirted them as though they were guard posts. The base appeared as big as a town, and I wondered where the hell we were going. The parade ground seemed miles behind. In fact, it was an accurate four hundred yards. We reached the dark corner of a barracks block by means of a crouching run, and squatted in its shadow, and:

'This is it,' Charlie said.

We were looking across a narrow concrete road. Over on the other side, a uniform row of look-alike houses were backed by a screen of tall trees. The houses, each with its own unfenced garden, were bordered by small well-trimmed shrubs. Everything neat and orderly.

'Married quarters,' I said. 'Officers', by the looks of 'em.'

'Number seventeen,' Charlie said. 'It's got to be the one with the lights on.'

'I think you are right,' Willy said.

'Damn right, I'm right.'

We were talking in whispers. 'So what happens now?' I said.

'We wait for five past nine,' said Willy.

'It's five past *now*!' Charlie said.

The road in front of us was eerily deserted all along its length, and due to a paucity of lighted windows, shrouded in murky gloom. When Willy checked his watch again, I instinctively looked at my own. Exactly seven minutes past nine.

'Jesus!' Charlie said. My thighs were aching, and I could well imagine what his must be feeling like. The drizzle was light, but steady and chilling. Our coats were becoming wet, and my hair was wet, and my feet felt wet.

'Jesus *Christ*!' Charlie said.

'It will be all right,' said Willy.

'One more minute,' Charlie said, 'and then we're going in there.'

'Charles, wait.'

'Wait, my arse!' Charlie said.

Even as he said it, something happened at the house across the way. An outside porch-light flicked on, and off.

'I told you,' Willy said. 'That was Kramer's signal.'

'All right, so let's go,' Charlie said.

We straightened up, with a cracking of knee-joints, and walked across the road to the house with lights behind its curtained windows. I fought a desire to run. But our presence on the road raised no alarm, and nobody started shooting at us. We might have been crossing a street on a dreary wet evening in a suburb of Harrogate. The glass-panelled door was standing ajar, darkness in the hall beyond. When the three of us were safely inside: 'Shut it,' Charlie said. I closed the door behind us and the hall, which was not very large, was suddenly filled with the smell of damp raincoats. 'Now, let's have some light.'

The man who switched on the overhead light was big except for his face. His head was in proportion, but the features belied its size. Small button eyes set close together across a snitch of a nose, and a purse-like mouth above a nothing of a chin. An M.P.'s uniform, sergeant's stripes on the shirt-sleeves, Colt's .45 on his hip. He was sweating profusely. He looked shit-scared.

'Sergeant Kramer,' said Willy.

'Where've you got Dorf?' Charlie said.

Kramer inclined his head sideways. 'In here.'

'Lead the way,' Charlie said.

The dining-room furniture was standard military. Cheap, but adequate. Table and chairs and sideboard, awful framed prints on the walls, and a serving-hatch for access to the kitchen. Floor covering wall-to-wall which might, at a pinch, be mistaken for Wilton. The table, set for four, was an unsightly litter of dishes and plates besmeared with remnants of food, and empty wine bottles and half-empty glasses. Charlie surveyed the scene, and all three men who were part of it. The two in uniform were very obviously out for the count. One sagged limp on his chair, the other one sprawled face-down across the table. The third man seemed half asleep. Half asleep, or totally drunk.

'Some party,' Charlie said.

'We must hurry,' said Willy, 'there isn't much time.'

'Time enough,' Charlie said, 'so long as they've had what you reckon they've had.'

'The dose was exact,' Willy said. He turned to Kramer. 'You gave it to them?'

'Just like you said,' Kramer said. 'Two each to the grunts, an' one to Dorf.'

'Right. Get stripped,' Charlie said.

Kramer said, 'Hey! Whaddya mean, "Get stripped"?'

'Get your gear off,' Charlie said, 'including gun and gaiters.'

'What is this?' Kramer said. His appeal was to Willy. 'What the *hell* is this?'

'Do as he says,' Willy said.

69

'Who is this guy?'

*'Just do as he says.'*

'Lissen! We had us a deal!'

Charlie ignored these inconsequentials. 'You—' he was talking to me. No names, no pack-drill. '—See to it.'

'You heard the man,' I said, 'so how do you want it? Hard, or easy?'

'Jesus!' Kramer said, but he started to unbutton his shirt.

'Shake it up,' Charlie said. He still had his hands in his raincoat pockets. Willy kept looking at his watch, as though willing the hands to stay where they were. I was undressing Dorf. It was just like changing a baby's nappy, except the baby weighed fifteen stone. He was fully conscious, but his mind was on holiday. His limbs seemed to weigh a ton. I didn't know then which drug had been used, and I still don't wish to know. You turn a blind eye, and keep it turned. That, or sweat out your dreams.

With Dorf dressed up in Kramer's uniform, including white helmet and gun, Charlie ground his teeth, and nodded. 'Willy?'

'Yes?' Willy said.

'Give Sergeant Kramer his happy pills.'

'Lissen!' Kramer said. He looked flabby and pathetic in his underwear. 'This has gotta look *good*!'

Willy took a brown plastic phial from his pocket and tipped out two yellow pills. 'Take these now, with some whisky.'

'They don't look the same!' Kramer said. 'I mean, not the same as I gave to the others!'

'They are just the same,' Willy said, 'except a little bit weaker. We need to be sure, you see, that all of you recover at about the same time.'

*       *       *

We moved at normal walking pace, with Charlie leading the way. Willy and I had Dorf between us, half-supporting him, and I got the side with the gun on the hip. The damn thing kept bumping my thigh. But Dorf was fairly quick to recover when exposed to the chill fresh air, and by the time

70

we were approaching the parade ground he was physically well-composed. Physically, but not mentally. He seemed unaware of his own identity—much less that of ours—or where he was, or what he was doing. We encountered not a soul, no roving patrols, not even a stray cat. Whatever Security there was, it must have been concentrated around the perimeter and down there at the main gates. I wondered how Ursula was faring with the sergeant in charge of the cars, and if she was managing to keep him occupied. In the line of duty, of course.

Mercifully, the rain had quickened. It was drumming on the roofs of cars and obscuring the view from windscreens and windows. Puddles were beginning to form all across the blacktop parade ground. As we splashed our way to the Rolls, I no longer imagined my feet were wet. I knew beyond all doubt.

'Christ, they don't make shoes like they used to.'

'Keep quiet, you twat!' Charlie said. Then, 'Got the stuff ready, Willy?'

'I have it here,' Willy said.

'Right. Hand it over, then get in your motor.'

'Be careful,' Willy said. 'Intra-muscular, *not* in a vein.'

He passed a small object to Charlie, and it required no genius to guess what it was they were talking about. I was aware of Willy slipping into the Mercedes, without actually seeing him get in. I was far too preoccupied in scanning the carpark, and striving to control a fibrillating sphincter muscle. How we got away with it, I do not know to this day, but Charlie had nerve enough for both of us.

'Open the boot,' he said. 'Not all the way. Just unlatch it, and hold it.'

We were standing at the back of the Rolls. Willy's Mercedes was parked on our right, and the car on our left appeared to be deserted. There were no cars parked behind, just an empty expanse of wet tarmac. I released the latch on the boot. Dorf was between us, out of this world, and soon to be further out. Charlie turned him around so that his back was to the Rolls. As I sprang, and held down, the boot lid, Charlie was jabbing a pre-filled hypodermic into Dorf's upper left arm. Now it wasn't merely raining, it was

71

absolutely pelting down.

'We'll never pull this one off, Charlie.'

'Get him in there,' he said.

Getting Dorf into the boot was so easy, I began to think it might work. He collapsed like a puppet against the back bumper, and when I raised the boot lid, all we needed to do was to tuck in his legs.

'Now shut it,' Charlie said, 'and get your coat off, and get in the car.'

The whole thing took less than one minute. We shed our tell-tale wet coats, and ducked in on either side of the Rolls.

'Jesus wept!' I said.

'Never mind "Jesus", sort yourself out.' He was drying the tight waves of his hair on one of his many white handkerchiefs.

'We might have been seen,' I said.

'Well, if we were, we'll soon find out.'

'It's all right for you mate,' I said, 'but I've got a poorly old dog back at home.'

'How awful.'

'Bollocks,' I said. 'I'm telling you, Charlie—'

'You're telling me nothing. And get your hair combed,' he said.

'We'll never get away with it. Any minute now—'

Charlie glanced at the dashboard clock. 'Any *second* now, our man will be getting a telephone call summoning him back to the toil.'

'But what if they search the car at the gate?'

'They didn't search it coming in.'

'And what if somebody checks on the house?'

'I told you to comb your hair. You look like a bloody porcupine.'

So then I said no more. In for a penny, in for a pound. Once committed, no turning back. Like landing a kite on a pitching ship after one abortive approach and with only about a pint of petrol in the tank. You do it, or you don't, and if you don't you are in the drink anyway. Hobson's choice.

'Shit!' I said. 'But I still don't like it, Charlie!'

'You don't have to like it,' he said. 'You just have to keep a

72

tight bum-hole.'

The bugger seemed at ease, quite relaxed. Me, I was plagued and tormented by a sudden farrago of thoughts, such as why was Dorf so loosely guarded? Kramer was, patently, a dolt. A sergeant only by dint of long service. If Dorf was so enormously valuable, they should have had him flown out and stashed him along with the gold in Fort Knox, not in an unguarded house at a barracks in vulnerable Germany. The Americans might appear to be naive, but they are never so naive as all *that*. These and other questions churned around in my mind, but Charlie appeared to be dozing. I just sat there and sweated, expecting at any time to hear the sounds of alarm and furore. The heavy shower had passed over, but the drizzle had now formed a mist, and I switched on the windscreen wipers.

'Switch them things off,' Charlie said.

'Sorry, Chas. I thought you were sleeping.'

'You know what Thought did,' he said.

So I switched off the wipers and sat there in silence. With an unconscious man in the boot, and a propensity towards diarrhoea. This is the unvarnished truth. Charlie had been my guide and mentor over most of twenty-five years. One quarter of a century, which represents one third of any reasonable life-expectancy. I pondered again on this fact as I sat there for what seemed like an aeon. Five minutes which seemed like five years. After a further year-long minute:

'Wake up, Charlie,' I said. He was instantly alert. 'There's somebody coming.'

White helmet and long yellow oilskin cape streaked by the endless rain. Big flashlight ranging across the parked cars, searching for a black Rolls-Royce with a Union Jack on its bonnet.

'Window,' Charlie said.

I let down my window, and the M.P. peered in. 'You the car for Sir Anthony Forbes?'

'That's us,' I said. 'What's the problem?'

'He's leaving,' the M.P. said.

'Not without us, he isn't.'

'That's right, so get down there,' he said. 'You seen Sergeant Harris?'

So that was his name. 'Sergeant who?' I said.

'Harris.'

'Sorry, can't help you.'

'Makes no matter,' he said, 'but you better get yoreselves down there. I been sent to tell you to *move*.'

'Thank you, soldier.'

'Thank *you*, sir.'

As he turned away, I fired the mighty engine.

'Take it easy,' Charlie said.

'Easy? You've got to be kidding!'

'Nice and gently,' he said.

I tooled the Rolls up close alongside of the steps to the officers' mess, and left the motor running. After a little time, which seemed to me to be a very long time, our man emerged from the door sheltered by a huge black umbrella held solicitously over him. He never addressed a word to us as he was ushered into the back, and when the door clunked behind him, shutting out the whole world, Charlie said:

'Right. Take it easy.'

'Tell me something new,' I said.

One small anxious moment at the gate, but nothing to sweat about. Then, as I drove along the thoroughfares of Frankfurt, 'We've done it Charlie,' I said. 'Jesus Christ, we've actually done it!'

\* \* \*

'Take the next left.'

'We'd be going the wrong way.'

'I said turn left,' Charlie said.

I touched the brake, and made a left turn. Our passenger ensconced in the back, isolated by a thick glass partition, seemed resigned to whatever we might do. A diplomat following Special Orders. Act thus, and do this, or that, or forget about a seat in the House of Lords. I hated that element of it all, but my hate was subjugated by my liking for living, to the business of staying alive. The street into which I turned was flanked by façades of up-market shops whose windows were brightly lit, with lavish displays of expensive goodies. All closed, at this time of night, but full

74

of the promise of an opening tomorrow.

'Turn left at the top,' Charlie said.

'Listen,' I said, 'where the hell are we going?'

'Just turn left,' Charlie said, 'and then next right, and right again.'

The Rolls slid around the corners as though the corners did not exist, but I couldn't stop thinking about the man in the boot. I knew that he wouldn't be bruised, because the great car made only soft rocking motions no matter what spin of the wheel. All I need do was follow instructions.

'Okay, stop here,' Charlie said.

A one-way street barely wide enough to allow the passage of a car, so I was forced to brake behind a BMW which blocked the narrow way. I was driving on sidelights only, but there was enough illumination to see that the dark-coloured car was silent and empty. Or so it appeared to be, but with vapour still wisping up off its bonnet.

'Right, then. Out,' Charlie said.

In any such human enterprise, timing is everything. Get the timing wrong, you can kiss it goodbye. Logistics too, of course, which was why this BMW had been left in this quiet street by someone just following orders, someone who might never know the purpose of the exercise.

Charlie stepped out of the car, and as I did likewise, 'What now?' I said.

'Help me get lover-boy switched over.'

'And what happens then?' I said.

'You drive the man back, and you get yourself a taxi.'

'A taxi to where?' I said.

'A taxi back to your girl friend's place—*and don't hang about!*' Charlie said. 'Half an hour, forty minutes at most.'

'Oh, thanks very much,' I said, 'but I don't even know where the hell I am!'

'First right, second left,' he said, 'and two more rights and you're down to the consulate. His Nibs will tell you the way.'

'That's great,' I said, 'that's just marvellous. So all I have to do—'

'All you have to do, is do as you're told.'

'Just like that,' I said.

'Correct. Just like that.'

So I helped him lug Dorf's limp body out of the boot of the Rolls and into the back of the BMW. We dumped him on the floor of the car, out of sight to any casual observer. I took most of the weight, and the effort left me out of breath.

'All right, then, Charlie,' I gasped. 'I'll see you back at Ursula's.'

'Get your skates on,' he said.

*     *     *

After I'd driven our man to the consulate, and was scouring the streets for a cab, I looked at my watch and I couldn't believe it. Only eleven o'clock. I had suffered a lifetime in the space of one evening. Barely three hours had passed since we entered the U.S. barracks. Unbelievable. Then, I had difficulty in getting a taxi. The first three drivers I stopped didn't want to know about a trip out to Kronberg. The buggers are all the same. London cabbies hate to cross bridges. Those plying north of the Thames will ask a fortune for a fare to Waterloo. When I finally did get a cab, it cost me such a lot of money I just knew I would never get it back from that miserable bastard in Section Accounts. Herr von Witherspoon would sniff, and push up his half-moon spectacles, and with just one stroke of his pen dismiss my claim as 'creative expenses'. James Bond, pack your bags. You have no conception of mundane reality.

I directed my cabbie to the little *Gasthaus* on Kronberg 2's market square, and when I was sure he had driven away I turned to trudge up the hill on the half-mile climb to Ursula's flat. The parking spaces out front were bereft of any BMW. I walked across the road to the church and scouted around in the dark, and there it was. Bonnet still warm from a heated engine, in spite of the cooling rain. I shrugged up the collar of my sad wet raincoat and recrossed the narrow road and walked down the path at the side of the flats to get to the door at the back. I was scared without knowing why, but nothing happened. Nothing at all. I touched the bell very briefly, and when Charlie opened the door I nipped inside, and said:

76

'Where's Ursula?'

'Never mind Ursula,' he said, 'are you sure you weren't tailed out here?'

'Positive. Where's Dorf?'

'Where the hell do you think? He's in the bedroom.'

'How did you manage him?'

'Never mind. What took you so long?'

'What took me so long,' I said, 'was trying to get a taxi on a rainy night.' I took off, and shook out, my Burberry. I felt wet, and chilled to the bone. I wanted a chair, and a very large malt with Malvern water, no ice. I wanted my slippers and my dog at my feet and a good log fire in the grate and something decent on the telly. 'When are the others due back?'

'Who cares? As soon as Dorf's mobile, we're leaving, and the others are on their own. No skin off their nose, no skin off ours.'

'Simple as that,' I said.

'Simple as that.'

'Don't tell me we don't still have problems.'

'Yes, of course we do, but we're over the big one.'

'Are we?'

'Farrow, you worry too much.'

'Yes, I know. You've told me before.'

'So how many more times?' he said.

'Besides, we need rest. You look knackered.'

'Listen, you speak for yourself—and don't get settled, start packing.'

'Packing? Give over!' I said. 'It's nearly midnight, and we both need a kip!'

'I told you, we're getting out. We're leaving before the shit hits the fan.'

'What about Willy and the girl?'

'What about 'em? Get your gear packed.'

'Balls. No way,' I said. 'I'm not about to shift until I know they're okay.'

'You're asking for it! You know?'

'Asking for what? A severe reprimand? Loss of pension rights? *What* bloody pension rights? Do me a favour!'

He fixed me with one of his stares, and when he realised I

77

was adamant, 'All right, calm down,' he said. 'We'll give 'em an hour.'

'No we won't, we'll give 'em as long as it takes.'

'In that case, get your bloody self shaved.'

'There's no hot water,' I said.

'What's wrong with boiling a kettle?'

'Christ, you can't win,' I said.

I was half inclined to argue, but in fact that shave I had then was highly conducive to quiet reflection. Not the narcissistic kind, absolutely no pun intended. As I was scraping my face, I reflected upon the events of the evening. Somehow, nothing seemed *right*. Dorf attended by second-class minders? With no apparent restraints? An ordinary house, no bars on its windows, no smell of an outside patrol, and evidence of Dorf's being at ease with his captors? A prisoner? No way. I wiped my face, and wiped the mirror, and looked at myself in the glass and pondered upon these matters.

'Listen, Charlie,' I called, 'I want to ask you something...'

'It'll have to wait,' he said, 'your girl friend's back.'

'Who—Ursula?'

'How many have you got here?' he said.

I heard the inner door open, and close, and then I heard Ursula say, 'Where is Marcus?'

'Relax,' Charlie said, 'we're all back safe and sound. Where's Willy?'

'He is parking the car.'

'Were you followed?'

'No.'

'Are you sure?'

'Yes, I am sure. We were not followed.'

'All right, then,' Charlie said. 'A quick cup of tea, and then we'll be off.'

'Off? Off where?' she said.

I was in the bathroom, buttoning up my shirt, but I could hear every word of it all.

Charlie said, 'None of your business.'

'Ignore him, luv,' I said.

Ursula spun round at the sound of my voice, and '*Gott sei*

*Danke!*' she said. Her face was flushed with excitement, or something, and her copper-glinting hair was bejewelled by crystal globules of rain which sparkled in the light like gems. I wanted to hug her, and kiss her forehead. Instead, I just winked at her.

'Any signs of disturbance when you left the barracks?'

'No, no. Nothing,' she said. 'All was perfectly normal.'

'Good. That's fine,' Charlie said.

'Any trouble with your sergeant?'

Ursula turned away, ostensibly to take off her coat. 'Only a little,' she said. I could well imagine the understatement.

'You did a good job,' Charlie said.

'Charles,' I said, 'you're a perfect gent.'

'You get yourself dressed,' he said. What he meant was *put a tie on*. I opened my mouth to reply, but he silenced me with a glare and a gesture which made me hold my breath. In the short fraught silence which followed we heard tiny scratchings at the door, small sounds of a key sliding into the lock. I could have sworn I never took my eyes off Charlie, but he suddenly had a gun in his hand. A Colt's .45, U.S. Army issue. He motioned me to take up the stance, back against the wall by the door. As we adopted the classic positions:

'It's Willy,' Ursula said.

And of course it *was* Willy, but it might *not* have been. I don't think he saw the gun, because it disappeared instantaneously.

'Come in, Willy,' Charlie said. 'We'd just begun to wonder what was keeping you.'

'A routine check,' Willy said, 'but we're clean. We're clean as a whistle.'

'I should hope so,' Charlie said.

As Willy shrugged out of his raincoat, 'It went beautifully, Charles,' he said. 'Everything easy, smooth as silk.'

'Smooth as silk,' Charlie said.

Ursula said, 'I will get us some drinks.'

'A brandy, please,' Willy said.

Charlie said, 'And we'll have some tea.'

'One tea, one whisky,' I said, 'and make the whisky a

large one.'

'Jesus Christ!' Charlie said, but I didn't give a monkey's. Ursula grinned at me, and went away into the kitchen. 'Right, then,' Charlie went on, 'all we need now is one more small favour.'

'No more favours, my friend. We had a firm arrangement.'

'Yes, I know,' Charlie said, 'but we can't just *walk* away from here. We need to borrow your car.'

'Borrow my car? That's impossible!'

'Give over!' Charlie said. 'We both know it's untraceable.'

'That is not the point! We had an arrangement!'

'Okay. So we'll keep Dorf here until such time as we can organise transport.'

'But you cannot keep Dorf here!'

'Come on, Willy. Make up your mind. What do you want us to do? Call for a bloody taxi?'

'*Scheisse*, man!' Willy said.

This was becoming curiouser and curiouser, as Alice was wont to say. Like why should Charlie want Willy's BMW, when we already had one of our own? But just as there is a time to speak out, there is likewise a time to shut up, so I just sat back and twiddled my thumbs. I would have liked to have gone to join Ursula in the kitchen, help her with the drinks, but this here was something I didn't want to miss. There was something going on that so far, I hadn't been told about.

'What's the big deal?' Charlie said. 'You lend us your car, we leave it at Helmstedt.'

'Helmstedt!'

'That's right,' Charlie said. 'We're making the swap at Marienberg.'

'But you said it was to be in Berlin!'

'No, I never. I never did.'

'But *Helmstedt*!' Willy said.

'Why not?' Charlie said. 'Friedrichstrasse's been overworked. Too much publicity. Marienberg's nice and quiet.'

'Even so,' Willy said, 'I cannot do it. I just can't do it.'

'Of course you can,' Charlie said. 'Think of the only

alternative.'

'*Gott in Himmel!*' Willy said.

'Forget about God in Heaven. What's it going to be?'

'Charles, I tell you, you are going too far!'

'Make up your mind,' Charlie said.

Poor Schumacher. What the hell could he do? 'Very well, then,' he said. 'Here are the keys, you may take my car.'

'I knew you'd see sense,' Charlie said. 'We'll leave it in front of that *Gasthaus*—remember it?'

'How could I forget?' Willy said. [See *The Leipzig Manuscript.*]

Ursula came in with her tray, and as I reached for my whisky, 'Go and check Dorf,' Charlie said.

I carried the tumbler with me, and took a soothing pull as I looked at Dorf lying there on the bed. He was sprawled out flat on his back, in the attitude of crucifixion. Arms spread wide, feet crossed, head lolled sideways, chin on chest. He was breathing stertorously, mouth wide open. He still wore the uniform, but Charlie had taken off the white helmet. It lay on the now-empty holster. Aside from his comatose condition, our prize was alive and well, and thus I reported to Charlie.

'He's still out cold,' I said, 'but his breathing's strong, and his colour seems okay.'

'So he's in good nick,' Charlie said.

'I wouldn't know. I'm not a doctor.'

'You surprise me,' Charlie said.

He was sipping the sort of tea he hated. Too weak, and too much milk, and infused by water left to go off the boil. Willy's brandy glass was just that little bit short of empty. Charlie had a curious effect on otherwise-uninhibited drinkers. Which, actually, Willy was *not*. I suddenly remembered that normally he drank nothing stronger than wine.

'He will be unconscious for two more hours, but you have a long way to go,' Willy said.

'Trying to get rid of us, are you?'

'No, but you yourself said—'

'I know what I said. Sup your poison.'

'Now listen, Charles—!'

'Yes?' Charlie said.

Willy's exasperation manifested itself in a sigh, and he drained his glass and handed it to Ursula. She rose and took it away, presumably to get him a refill.

'I forgot something,' Charlie said.

Lying bugger, he never forgot anything.

'What is it now?' Willy said.

'Gear for Dorf, civilian gear. We can't swap him as he is, in U.S. Army uniform.'

'Quite right. It's not done,' I said.

Willy cast me a stricken glance. I had made it two against one. The neutral observer turned aggressor.

'But surely you *planned* this thing!'

'One of those little oversights, Willy.'

Oversight. That was a laugh. He had seen an advantage, *in situ*, and grasped it. How better to stroll through the base than accompanied by a military policeman?

'Look at it this way,' I said. 'The uniform helped get us all free and clear. We're pure as the driven snow.'

'Free and clear, and pure as snow?'

'Farrow's right,' Charlie said.

Which put the ball back in *my* court. 'So it's no big problem,' I said. 'A pair of trousers and a roll-neck sweater, a jacket and a coat, and Bob's your Uncle. We're home and dry.'

'Home and dry,' Willy said. Much depended on his co-operation. Charlie's clothes wouldn't fit Dorf, and I never carry excess baggage. 'This is too much!' he went on.

Charlie just shrugged, so it was left to me. 'Nothing to it,' I said. 'You must have a bloke around about Dorf's size— around my size.'

'That is not the point,' Willy said.

Charlie said, 'Willy, you're repeating yourself.'

'Now then, let's be fair,' I said.

I actually smelled Willy's resentment; it charged the atmosphere. But he and Charlie were two of a kind. Me, I'd have blown my top, and told us both to go and get stuffed. As it was, Willy's nostrils turned white, and his tea-coloured eyes seemed to glow dull red.

'What more?' he almost hissed. 'First the car, and now the

clothes.'

'Oh, nothing more,' Charlie said. His tone was mild as mothers' milk. 'Farrow?'

'No,' I said, 'I think that's just about everything.'

'Everything,' Willy said. Ursula must have been listening in the hall, waiting for the opportune time to enter and avert an embarrassment. She handed Willy his drink, and he looked at Charlie over the rim of the glass as he took a hefty snort. He wiped his lips on the tips of three fingers. 'This is the very last thing. I will use the phone in the bedroom.'

'Be our guest,' Charlie said. 'Watch out for the Sleeping Beauty.'

I stared at him, shaking my head, but he blandly ignored the implied reproof. We heard Willy mumbling on the phone, and when he rejoined us he said, 'Twenty minutes.'

'More tea, then?' Ursula said.

Charlie said, 'Farrow will get it.' Farrow would be only too pleased. I took his mug and moved towards the kitchen. As I reached the sitting-room door, 'And *you*,' he went on, 'no more boozing. You've got a long drive ahead.'

Ursula followed me into the kitchen. 'Your boss is very rude.'

'That's the nicest thing anybody ever said about him.' I put the kettle on to boil. 'Could I have another spot of whisky?'

'Of course, but . . .'

'Sod him,' I said.

I drank my bonus drop of Scotch as I was stewing Charlie's tea. From somewhere close within the building, a dog began to bark. The excited yapping of a small one, a terrier.

'That is Schatzi,' Ursula said, 'Jutta's dog. My neighbour.'

'Ah, your friend from next door,' I said. 'She must be getting a welcome home.'

'I doubt it,' Ursula said, 'she almost always goes to bed early.'

'Somebody else coming home?'

'No. Unless one is extra careful, the outer door makes a noise.' I felt a sudden freezing of the hairs on the back of my neck. Ursula read the thought on my face, and clamped a hand on my wrist. 'You do not think . . .'

'Not really . . . but *maybe*.'

I glanced at the kitchen clock. The time was twenty past midnight.

'I knew it,' said Willy, 'I felt it in my bones.'

'Bullshit,' Charlie said. He looked to Ursula. 'This neighbour of yours—can she keep her mouth shut?'

'Of course!'

'And have you still got that key to her flat?'

'We always have each other's keys.'

Charlie was polishing, again, his spectacles. 'Right, then, here's what to do. This could be a big nothing, but get yourself over there, and spin her a yarn. If she's got any lights on, make sure you switch 'em all off. Listen for your colleague bringing the gear for Dorf. Catch him before he starts ringing this bell.'

'I understand,' Ursula said. 'You mean, make it appear that he's coming to see Jutta?'

'You've got it,' Charlie said. 'Then, wrap yourself up so you can't be recognised, and take the dog for a walk.'

'Jesus,' I said, 'she's not stupid, Charlie! You don't need to spell it out.'

He carried on as though I'd not spoken. 'Take the pooch round the block. You know what I mean?'

'Yes, I know what you mean.'

'I will do it,' Willy said.

'No you won't! Christ Almighty!' For once, I agreed with him. Willy must be going soft in the head. If there *was* an Element out there, that Element had probably been briefed about the occupants of every flat in the building. 'Sure you've got it?' Charlie went on.

'Yes, I've got it. I know what to do.'

'Right, then. Off you go.'

Ursula put on a big loose coat, wound a scarf around her head, and checked that she had the proper keys.

'You take care, kid,' I said. We listened for the opening and closing of doors, but heard almost no sound at all. 'Ursula's good.'

'Let's bloodywell hope so.'

'Now listen—!' Schumacher said.

85

'Farrow, get Willy some more of his medicine.'

Willy covered his glass with his hand. 'No. No more.'

'Had enough of it, have you?'

'Jesus, Charlie!' I said.

'You, sit down. You're a blot on the landscape.'

'Up-your-gunga,' I said.

But I perched on a chair, and we sat then in silence, listening for noises outside. When at last we heard the latch of the outer door, Charlie held up a hand. Ursula must have been waiting for him out there in the cold dark hall. Next came a buzzing of next door's bell, followed by a pause, followed by a mumble of voices. Another, longer, pause, and then a muted banging of doors as Ursula went out with the dog. Had I been a religious man, I might have breathed a prayer. I thought about it, anyway. Charlie sipped cold tea from his mug. Willy chewed his lips, nursing, like me, an empty glass. Five minutes . . . seven minutes . . . ten . . .

'*Scheisse!*' Willy whispered. 'What has happened to her?'

'Nothing,' Charlie said. 'She's just doing what she was told to do.'

'Told by *you!*' Willy said. 'I'm warning you, Charlie. I am warning you—'

'Save your breath,' Charlie said.

I kept my mouth shut. Silence is golden. But it worried the hell out of me that Ursula should be taking so long. As someone once rightly said: It's not the war, it's the waiting.

When eventually she did return, she let the outer door bang shut. To anyone who might possibly be interested her conduct was patently that of an irate woman roused late from her bed by an unexpected guest. Unexpected, and not very welcome. We heard raised voices next door, but only for two or three minutes, and I visualised lights being switched off. I imagined all three of them waiting until sufficient time had elapsed for any observers to have swallowed the deception.

'What is holding her up?' Willy said.

Charlie said, 'Keep your voice down.'

The scratching of a key in the door, and tiny sounds of it opening and closing. Then Ursula walked in, still wearing that coat and the wrap-around headscarf. She took it off, and shook out her hair and 'Two of them,' she said. 'One at the front, and one at the back.'

'Well, what d'you know?' Charlie said. 'The Cousins must be getting better.'

'The Americans?' Willy said.

Charlie said, 'Listen, are you sure only two?'

'Do you wish to go see for yourself?'

'That's the way. You tell him, luv.'

'And you watch your mouth,' Charlie said.

Willy said, 'Christ! They are on to us!'

'Are they hell as like,' Charlie said. 'All they're doing, they're covering all options.'

'And especially this one,' I said.

'Farrow, I told you to shut your gob.'

'But now we can't move Dorf!' Willy said.

'Of course we can. Just calm down, and listen . . .' The computer he used for a brain had been at work even as we were speaking. '. . . it's as simple as A,B,C. We can turn their suspicions to our advantage.'

'I would like to know how,' Willy said.

Charlie was looking to Ursula. 'This friend of yours,' he said, 'how far do you think you can trust her?'

'I would trust her with my life.'

'Your life is what we're talking about.'

'She is totally reliable.'

Uncharitably, I thought of Sappho. 'Ursula, lass,' I said, 'you have to be very sure about that.'

'You finished now?' Charlie said. 'I'm talking to the young lady.'

'And I'm talking to you,' I said. 'Whatever you're thinking, it better be good.'

'Farrow is right,' Willy said.

'Well, if you're both done—'

'Go on,' said Ursula.

She had taken off her coat, and was perched on the arm of the sofa. She looked so eager, and young, I feared for such vulnerability. I wasn't afraid for myself, I just wanted nothing to happen to her.

'All right, so let's hear it,' I said.

Charlie said, 'Just be quiet, Farrow.'

87

'Never mind the crap. Tell us what you've got in mind.'

'I will second that,' Willy said.

As Charlie rearranged his clothing, 'What we have here,' he said, 'is a very simple situation. We must get Dorf out of this flat, so he goes next door, care of Willy's minder.'

'Oh yes, and what then?' I said.

'We sit here and wait for Westerholme.'

'Westerholme?' I said. 'What the hell has he got to do with it?'

'Everything,' Charlie said, 'he's Head of Station—'

'He's down in Munich.'

'*Was* down there,' Charlie said, 'but you can bet your life he's on his way back. He'll have got the word about Dorf, and Dorf is bigger than both of us. Besides, if he hasn't smelled a rat, he must be even thicker than we thought.'

'So you think he'll come here?' I said.

'No, I don't think so. I know so.'

'What makes you so sure?' Willy said.

'Because he knows this place was our base of operations.'

'You mean, he *knows* we took Dorf?'

'No, not at all. But we're his best bet. We fooled him into leaving town, and how long d'you suppose it would take him to realise—'

'Okay. So he hears about Dorf, rides an Air Force jet out of Munich, arrives here before he departs, and drives like hell up to Kronberg?'

'That's right. You want to bet?'

'So why the hell are we keeping Dorf here?'

'We're not. We're shifting him next door.'

'You sure about this? Do you know what you're saying?'

I could scarcely believe my ears. For Charlie to use a civilian was a rare phenomenon, one thing he always tried to avoid.

But, 'Move yourself,' he said. 'Get Dorf next door—and Willy, you go with him. Tell your man to switch clothes, make Dorf ready for moving out. Leave the uniform where it is.'

'I do not like it.'

'Nobody likes it, but you got a better idea?'

The struggle to get Dorf slung over my shoulder made me

realise how tired I was. We had been on the go since seven a.m., best part of eighteen hours, and we sure as fate weren't getting any younger. As Willy gathered up the gear—white helmet and webbing and so forth—Ursula was tidying up the bed. She smoothed down the counterpane then stood back to check, biting the tip of a thumb.

'Ye . . e . . s, I think that is everything.'

'Right. Lead the way,' I said.

She went on ahead of us, opening doors very quietly. The loudest sounds I heard were those of my own stifled gasping. Dorf seemed to weigh five tons. I humped him across the dimly-lit lobby and into the flat opposite. Ursula's friend—just a shape in the darkness—guided me into a room, and I lowered my burden onto a bed. As the girl led me out, I could hear Willy's rapid whisperings as he told his man what to do. Ursula dealt with the doors again, and we were all back into her flat within not much more than one minute. I was still breathing hard. Charlie nodded towards a chair.

'Sit down before you collapse.'

'Yes, and you know what *you* can do!'

'Cheeky.'

'Bollocks!' I said. His frown of reprimand made me feel guilty, because of course it doesn't do to reveal such discord in the presence of third parties. So, 'Sorry,' I went on, 'but I'd just like to know the rest of it.'

'The rest of it,' Charlie said, 'is perfectly simple and straightforward. Any minute now, Willy and the girl and me and his laddo—representing *you*—are going to get out of here using both cars. The Cousins are bound to tail us, because what can be the point of watching a flat which they know to be empty?'

'But they won't know it's empty,' I said.

'They will after Westerholme's been here.'

'But we're not sure he's coming.'

'He'll come.'

We were embroiled by now in one of our charades. It was question-and-answer time. I asked the questions, and he gave the answers, and anyone looking on was usually persuaded that the whole thing was genuine.

'Well, assuming he does come,' I said, 'and assuming you lot lead them all away, what happens then?'

'No sweat. You get Dorf out, and you meet us at Hanau.'

'Impossible,' Willy said. 'Farrow will be left without a car.'

'He can use mine,' Ursula said.

'No,' Charlie said, 'we don't want you involved any more than you need to be. Farrow can "borrow" one, there's plenty outside.'

'Could be difficult,' Ursula said.

'Not for him. He's a congenital thief.'

I let that one go by. It was just his way of telling me to use the other BMW.

'Let's get this straight,' I said. 'You all go now, and leave me with Dorf—'

'That's correct,' Charlie said.

'—and at two o'clock, I get him out. Why wait until two o'clock?'

'Because that's when he should start to get ambulatory.'

'Ambulatory?' I said.

'Means he'll be able to walk, you dumb bastard. Unless you want to *carry* him out.'

'No, thanks. I'll wait until two o'clock.'

'Yes, I thought you might. So we'll see you in Hanau, in the Hauptbahnhof carpark, around about half past two.'

Hanau lay fifteen miles to the east.

'Sounds all right,' I said, '*if* the Cousins *do* follow you, and *if* you can lose 'em.'

'Christ, we're in two cars! If we can't lose the buggers in Frankfurt . . .'

'No problem,' Willy said. I think he was anxious to be rid of us.

'All satisfied?' Charlie said. 'Is everybody satisfied?' He looked at each of us, and when none of us gave him an argument, 'Right, that's it then,' he said.

\*      \*      \*

I don't think I would have minded if, just for once, he'd been wrong, but I might have known it was too much to hope for. When they came, at five to one, he and I were wearing our coats as though about to leave. We knew they would know we hadn't just arrived, because they'd had surveillance outside for at least an hour, and maybe more. We heard them enter the lobby, and were ready for a ring at the bell. When it came, Charlie nodded at Ursula, and 'Let 'em in,' he said.

Willy looked sad, and tired. He looked exactly like I felt. Ursula on the other hand looked bright-eyed and bushy-tailed, as if she had just embarked on the night-shift. When she let them in, they stood in the sitting-room doorway, and:

'Well, lookahere,' Westerholme said. 'If it ain't the old limey double-act.'

'Why, Westerholme!' Charlie said. 'What brings *you* here at this time of night?'

'Business,' Westerholme said. He was accompanied by only one of his minions. He had probably left the other one outside, with instructions to brief the two watchers.

'What business?' Charlie said. 'You'd better make it fast, because we're just about to leave.'

'No, you're not,' Westerholme said.

'Good,' I said, 'I'm glad to hear it. I could sleep on a bed o' nails.'

'A bed of nails is what you got.'

'Look, spit it out,' Charlie said.

Willy, in shirt-sleeves with necktie pulled loose, was lounging on the couch. Ursula cosied up beside him, and:

'Please—sit down,' she said.

'No, thanks. We'll stand.'

'Take a seat, Westerholme. You look a bit frayed.'

'Don't you worry about me.'

'Sorry I spoke.'

'That's the thanks you get, Farrow.'

'I'm used to it, Charlie,' I said.

'I thought you guys were going to Munich?'

'That's right, and we went,' Charlie said, 'and we've just got back—haven't we, Farrow?'

'Don't ask me,' I said, 'all this bloody jet-lag, I hardly know *where* we've been.'

'Munich lies south-east of here—'

'Is that a fact?' Charlie said.

'—and jet-lag occurs only west to east.'

'I thought it was east-west?' Charlie said.

'Every day you learn something new.'

'Farrow, how true,' Charlie said.

Westerholme smiled. 'Okay, play your games. But this time, *we* get the laughs.'

'Pity,' I said, 'I could do with a chuckle.'

'He's feeling sad,' Charlie said. 'He's worrying about his poorly old dog.'

'And that is the truth,' I said.

'You two got more to worry about than any poorly ole dog. You two jokers got much bigger problems.'

'Farrow, what *can* he mean?'

'I don't know. Were we speeding?'

'That's it!' Charlie said. 'He's moonlighting as a traffic cop!'

'Well, for Christ's sake plead guilty,' I said, 'and pay the ticket, and let's go home. I'm knackered.'

'Me too,' Charlie said, 'but we must observe the proper formalities.'

'Hands on heads!' Westerholme said.

'Hark at him, Willy. He's got a gun in his pocket.'

'I said, put your hands on your heads!'

Charlie kept his hands in his raincoat pockets, and I kept my hands in mine. Willy and Ursula were acting half-drunk. He was mustering a frown, and she was attempting to stifle a giggle. Charlie heaved a great sigh.

'Westerholme,' he said, 'for Christ's sake grow up. What the *hell* do you think you're on?'

'He thinks he's on his Daddy's yacht.'

'That's right, Farrow,' Charlie said, 'he thinks he's back home in them U.S. of A.'

'Little ole South Georgia,' I said, 'big tough sheriff, star on his chest.'

'Boss-man of all he surveys.'

'He thinks he's back there on his own stamping-ground.'

'I know where I am,' Westerholme said.

'In that case,' said Willy, 'would you mind telling *me* what it is that you're doing here?'

'Good for you, Willy. You *tell* him!'

'Yes, we're all Willy's guests,' Charlie said, 'so I think you owe it to him, Westerholme. Common courtesy.'

Had Westerholme not been tired, and furious, he might have played it differently. As it was, we had badgered him into a corner. He must pee, or get off the pot. Our four pairs of eyes watched him agonise. The silence, fraught and intense, was broken at last by Charlie.

'Come on, for Christ's sake,' he said. 'It's very late, and we've had a long day. What's your problem?'

'Okay. We're missing a warm body, and we think you guys have it.'

'*Warm body*?' Willy said. 'Charles, do you know what he's talking about?'

'Don't ask *me*,' Charlie said.

Westerholme snarled, 'Come off it, Willy! We know you were down at the base. You and this girl were down there tonight!'

'Base? *Was ist "base"*?' Willy said.

'At the party at the barracks in Frankfurt!'

'Ah, yes, of course!' Willy said. 'We were running security on General Kempf.'

'Are you telling us,' Charlie said, 'that this warm body you're chuntering about was lifted from a U.S. base?'

'Leave off, McGowan. Don't act so surprised.'

'Well, *I'm* surprised,' I said. 'Go on, Westerholme, this is fascinating!'

'Are you saying,' Willy said, 'that Ursula and I stole this body of yours? I must warn you to have a care!'

'Typical yankee balls-up. He's dropping himself right in the shit.'

'Charlie,' I said, 'this doesn't concern us.'

'Like hell it doesn't!' Westerholme said. 'You sonsabitches are up to your necks!'

'This is mad,' Willy said. 'Herr Westerholme, you are in serious trouble.' He sat up, and straightened his tie. 'I am going immediately to lodge a complaint.'

'Now, hang on,' Charlie said, 'we're all of us human, and we all make mistakes.' He looked to Westerholme. 'After

93

this, you're going to owe us both an apology. So tell us what's on your mind, and then piss off, and we might just forget it.'

'Sod that, Charlie!' I said, 'I'm not going to forget it.'

'Live and let live,' he said. 'If we can't give and take in this lousy business . . .'

'That's all very well,' I said, 'but this bugger's gone past the limit!'

'Westerholme, he's right,' Charlie said. 'So cough it up, get it all off your chest, and then we'll be on our way.'

I almost felt sorry for Westerholme. He gnawed at his lower lip, but having come this far, he had to go through with it.

'We're taking a look around.'

'Don't you think you should ask the lady's permission?'

'It is all right,' Ursula said. 'Let them do it, and then they might leave.'

Westerholme nodded at his mate, and the mate went off on a tour of the premises. It did not take very long, and when he came back, he shook his head.

'Satisfied?' Charlie said.

'Not hardly. What car are you driving?'

'We've borrowed Willy's,' Charlie said.

'Okay, so let's go an' take a look.'

'Tell him to sod off!' I said.

'I'm tempted, Farrow, but we better get this settled.'

'Damned right!' Westerholme said.

He and his mate came outside with us, and when Charlie unlocked the car, they both inspected the interior.

'Now, the trunk,' Westerholme said.

'What we have here is a sceptic.'

'A sceptic? A pillock!' I said.

Westerholme stared into the empty boot as though reluctant to believe his eyes. I sensed that his minion was now convinced they were chasing a very wild goose. He spoke for the first time.

'That's it then, chief. Looks like we got a bum steer.'

Westerholme rounded on Charlie and me. 'You two ain't out of this, yet!'

Charlie shrugged, and turned his back, and started to

94

walk away. As Westerholme moved to go after him, I put a hand on his arm.

'Give over. You've made a right fool of yourself.'

'Have I?'

'Yes,' I said. 'Look, it's raining, and we're all getting wet, so why don't you just go away and pursue a more fruitful line of enquiry?'

'You bastards think you're so smart!'

'No more than average, but you're on the wrong track. The job we came here to do has nothing whatever to do with your problem.'

'You bastards think you're so smart!'

'You said that before, and the answer's the same. So if you'll excuse me,' I said, 'I'll go and say goodbye to Willy.'

'We'll be watching you,' Westerholme said.

'Hey, come on! We're supposed to be allies.'

'Don't give me *that* shit!' he said.

\*       \*       \*

I wiped my hair on the sleeve of my coat.

'Have they all gone?' Willy said.

Charlie said, 'You've got to be joking.'

'Wes and his chum left,' I said. 'At least, they drove off.'

'*Gott!* I feel exhausted.'

'Don't we all,' I said.

Ursula said, 'I will make more coffee.'

'Forget it,' Charlie said. Then, to me, 'Are the others still out there?'

'I couldn't tell you,' I said. 'If they are, I didn't spot 'em.'

'Means bugger-all,' he said, 'you couldn't spot an elephant on a billiards table.'

'Thank you, *mein Führer*,' I said.

Ursula said, 'I will go take a look.'

'Don't bother,' Charlie said, 'they're out there sure as God made apples.'

'Little apples,' I said.

He took no notice. 'All right, let's get organised. Farrow, get Dorf back in here—and don't leave any Army gear behind.'

95

'I will help you,' Ursula said.

'Yes,' Charlie said, 'you do that—and tell that friend of yours to keep her mouth shut.'

'Jesus, Charlie!'

'Get on with it,' he said.

Had Willy's man not given me a hand, I'd have had a pretty tough time hoisting Dorf up over my shoulder. As we were getting him all set, Ursula groped around in the darkness to gather up the gear. She stuffed helmet and webbing and gaiters into a plastic shopping bag. Jutta, her friend, kept a very low profile. She crouched on the other twin bed, holding the little dog in her arms, and never uttered a word.

With Dorf safely back in Ursula's flat, 'So let us go!' Willy said.

'Just a minute.'

'What is it *now*, Charles?'

'I want a word with Farrow,' he said. I followed him into the bathroom, and he motioned me to shut the door. After he'd opened the wash-basin taps, 'Listen,' he went on, 'don't leave here until two o'clock. By the time you get to Hanau, I should be well shot of these buggers.'

'Christ, they're *helping* us, Charlie!' I said.

'Never mind, just do as I say.'

'All right, I heard you,' I said. 'But I'm not bloody driving all the way to Berlin. Not tonight, anyway.'

'All you have to do is get Dorf to Hanau.'

'You expect me to believe that?' I said.

\*     \*     \*

All four of them left, carrying mine and Charlie's luggage. Nobody said goodbye. I made no attempt to peep through the curtains, to see if the Cousins took the bait. They did, or they didn't. Either way, there was nothing I could do. Suddenly, the flat seemed empty, and menacing. I ran another check on Dorf, hoping for signs of movement. He was grunting like a heifer in calf and I wondered, again, what drug they had given him. It was twenty-five minutes past one. Another half-hour of nothing but waiting.

Waiting in the dark, because of course when they left they switched all the lights off. By tentative feeling, and touch, I fumbled a path to the kitchen and poured myself a small jar. It brought me no comfort. I lay on the couch with my head on one of its arms, and longed to surrender myself to sleep. I was aided in staying awake by the rhythmic snoring which came from the bedroom. The luminous hands of my watch measured off the minutes, each one of which seemed like an hour. At a quarter to two, I heard groanings and mumblings. Dorf was coming round. I heaved myself wearily upright, and bumping against furniture, groped my way into the bedroom. He was struggling to sit up, one hand propped behind him, the other clasping his brow.

'*Mein Gott! Mein Kopf!*' My God! My head!

'It's all right, Dorf,' I said. 'Take it easy. Everything's all right.'

'*Mein Gott!*'

'Lie down,' I said. 'Lie down, and take it easy, and I'll get you a drink of water—okay?'

'*Bitte schöen.*'

'Fine. I'll be back in one moment. Relax, you're safe now,' I said.

I went to fetch him a drink of water. In the dark, it took some little time, and when I got back he was heaving and retching. There was vomit all over the bed. I couldn't see it, but I could smell it, and feel it.

'O suffering Jesus!' I said.

'*Was ist los?*'

'Come on, sit up.'

Easier said than done. I supported him with an arm around his shoulders, and held the tumbler to his lips. He gulped at the water, but he couldn't keep it down. It erupted in a flood which further soiled himself and the bed and incidentally, me. I spent the next ten minutes or so trying to resuscitate Dorf. I heaved and hauled him up off the bed and into the sitting room, and got him seated at one end of the sofa. Then I swabbed at our clothes with a towel from the bathroom, but the stink of spew clung fast, and foul and persistent. Now here was a pretty mess such as Mr Gilbert never envisaged.

97

'Drink some more water,' I said. 'Force it down, swill your guts out.'

'What is happening?' he said.

'Never mind. Just do it.' I pressed the glass to his mouth, and he swallowed some more, and was sick again. 'That's the way,' I said, 'better than a bloody great tube down your throat.'

'Aaaargh . . . O, *Gott!*' he said.

Ursula's carpet was taking a beating. Everything in his stomach came up. All that he'd eaten down at the base was disgorged between his knees, and his groans would have moved the heart of Torquemada. They certainly moved mine, and as I wiped the sweat off his brow, 'Don't worry, you're safe now,' I said.

Unwittingly, I had spoken in English, and received a jolt of surprise when he answered me in that same language.

'Safe? What is safe?' he said. 'Where am I? Who are you? What has happened?'

I sneaked a glance at my watch. The illuminated dial showed five past two. Time to be moving on. Dorf would be able to walk, or stagger, but that small part of it all was not the part which worried me. I was, by now, quite convinced that our man was a willing defector. Not a prisoner, but a *guest* of the Yanks, and when he recovered his strength and his senses I was going to have a problem on my hands. All he had to look forward to was Siberia, or a hole in the head. By swapping this man for McKenzie, we were sentencing him to death.

So I sat with an arm around that miserable human being and tried to ease his distress, knowing that any comfort I gave was temporary, and false. The knowledge was distasteful. Few are ever called to weigh one man's life against that of another. Not merely called, but compelled. Solomon got it right with the baby, but his was just a smart-arse trick and this with Dorf was something less easy, infinitely more profound. I envied Charlie's simplicity of reason, his absolute unwavering belief that the greater evil justifies the lesser. To him, Dorf was only a pawn in a game whose stakes went far beyond checkmate. I forced myself to slow down. I made myself think about young McKenzie,

98

twice saviour of my life. Eager and earnest, but cool and calm when events roiled up to a crunch. Five hundred years of selective breeding, salt of this island earth. Spirit of Wallace, and Robert the Bruce, and Crécy and Agincourt and two world wars and the Falklands. *Et cetera.*

Mollified by such fanciful musings, I returned to reality. Dorf's stomach was just about empty, but he was torn by gut-wrenching heaves which brought up tenuous drools of slime. They strung from his chin and smelled diabolical.

'Take another drink,' I said.

Most men in such an awful condition will grasp at any straw, a fact for which I was truly thankful. I wanted him like that. I wanted him up on his feet, but complaisant and easy to handle, putty in my hands. I wanted him to be as he was down in Frankfurt; able to move himself without any care as to where he was going.

'Come on, Dorf, we're leaving,' I said.

'Leaving?'

'Yes. We have to go.'

'Go?'

'Yes. *Move!*' I said.

'I cannot think. I have terrible headache.'

'I understand,' I said, 'but we have to get away from here.'

'But I do not know where I am. Where is "here"? Where am I?'

'Never mind,' I said. I patted his back like patting a baby, which served to force up more bile. My arm supporting his shoulders had begun to feel heavy as lead, so I got both forearms under his armpits and heaved him up on his feet. The effort took just about all of my strength. His weight was equal to mine, and I wasn't at the top of my form. I was feeling far from my best. I felt old and weary, close to exhaustion. Groping in the dark, I pulled his right arm around my shoulders, grasped the wrist in my fist, and then with my left arm encircling his waist, stumbled him through two doors. Outside, the sudden chill of the night pierced me to the core. I wondered, briefly, if Ursula's close neighbour was awake and listening, but my main concern had to do with the Cousins. If Westerholme had left just one man . . .

I tried to abjure such negative thoughts as I mustered Dorf out the back and around the side and across the road to the carpark fronting the church. He seemed to have adopted the form of a life-sized rubber elephant each of whose wobbly legs was bent upon moving in separate directions, and I marvelled at the fact that Charlie, ill as he was, had managed to lug him from car to flat. The analogy of a nine-stone mother hoisting a one-ton car in order to free her trapped children flashed across my mind. Thought travels much faster than physical impulse. Faster, even, than light.

The world seemed unnaturally empty. Black, and silent, and still, the revellers in the flat upstairs fallen into their beds with a gentle rain to lull them to rest. *Too* quiet? *Que sera, sera.* What will be, will be. Terribly bad discipline, but I was almost past caring. I propped Dorf against the car, opened the door, and bundled him into the front passenger seat. He collapsed against the squab with his head lolled back, breathing noisily. I moved around the front of the bonnet, watching him through the screen, and dumped myself in the driving seat. As I started the engine, he groaned and said:

'*Was ist los?*'

'*Ist nichts,*' I said. 'Take it easy.'

He appeared to believe what I'd said, and as I drove out of Kronberg I took good care to make sure that nobody, but nobody, followed us. The roads swam before my eyes, but my hands on the wheel kept a link with reality. The end of my tether was near, and I knew I was drawing on final reserves, but the training swept me along with no regard to demands from the body. I followed the roadside signs and blessed that one which read HANAU, and the rest was blessed relief. The way to the station was clearly marked. No bother, no trouble at all. He was starting to get his act together. The drugs were wearing off, and I was worried as to how much he might be dissembling. The last thing I needed right now was for him to recover and become obstreperous. I offered a silent prayer.

The carpark at Hanau railway station lies at the back of the tracks, which are fronted by the booking office. Not much need for security, because the vast majority of its users commute into Frankfurt each day, parking in the morning and departing each evening. No call for surveillance at night, and so the lighting was minimal, just a token neon lamp at each of the carpark's four corners. So most of the lot was dark and deserted, only a few scattered cars forming darker shapes against a less-dark background. I switched the headlamps off, and drove in slowly on sidelights only, hunched forward over the wheel to peer through the rain-spotted windscreen. Charlie appeared like a wraith, looming up suddenly just short of the bonnet. As I jumped on clutch and brake, Dorf lurched forwards. His face hit the dashboard, and he loosed a strangled cry. Charlie moved up as I opened my door, and:

'You bloody near hit me,' he said.

'You jumped out in front, for Christ's sake!'

'Jesus! What's that stink?'

'You'd better get used to it, Charlie. Dorf's spewed all over himself.'

'Smells like *you* spewed all over yourself. Couldn't you—?'

'No!' I said, 'and don't start that crap, I've had enough with this bugger!'

'Calm down. Get him into the back.' He helped me lug Dorf out of the front seat and bundle him into the rear. 'Now get our bags. We haven't got all night.'

'What happened to Willy and the girl? And I thought we were leaving their car at Helmstedt?'

'You thought wrong. Shake it up!' By the time I had the gear transferred he was lodged in the driving seat, and he motioned me to sit in the back. 'Watch him—'

'Thanks very much.'

'—and if he starts to get stroppy, hit him.'

'I bloodywell knew it!' I said. 'Why didn't you *tell* me that Dorf was a runner?'

'And have you shit yourself? You've made enough stench around here as it is.'

'The Ivans will top this poor sod.'

'I don't give a chuff what they do with him.'

'Charlie, you're all heart,' I said.

With traffic virtually non-existent he ignored two or three red lights, and when we hit a large roundabout he followed an illuminated sign which pointed the way to Hannover and Braunschweig. The latter lay close to Helmstedt, but both were many miles hence, and the thought of a four- or five-hour journey filled me with dismay. Time was when a couple of nights without sleep were a concomitant of the job, but that time was past and beyond return. I felt near to the end of my rope, weary to the point of collapse. My eyelids were drooping fast, and it was all I could do to keep them open.

'Listen, Charlie,' I said, 'there's no way that either of us can stay awake to drive to Helmstedt tonight.'

'Who said anything about driving to Helmstedt?'

'But I thought—'

'You think too much. You ought to give over, you'll strain yourself.'

'So where *are* we heading for, then?'

'We're going up to Lübeck-Travemünde.'

'Lübeck? Jesus Christ!'

'Scene of your early triumph. One of your old stamping grounds.'

'Never mind the flannel, you're talking about three hundred miles!'

'Two hundred and forty. Don't exaggerate.'

'Exaggerate my arse! Drop me off at the next motel!'

'Keep your knickers on. We'll stop and have a kip in the car.'

'A kip in the car?' I said. 'And what about Sleeping Beauty? Suppose he gets his marbles back, and decides he's had enough of our company? What if he buggers off?'

'He won't bugger off without taking you with him.'

'Oh? How come?' I said.

Charlie took one hand off the wheel but he kept his eyes on the road as he grappled around in his raincoat pocket to come up, finally, with a pair of shiny steel handcuffs. Still with his eyes on the road, he dangled them over the back of the squab.

'Umbilical,' he said. 'One on your right wrist, the other on his left. He's left-handed.'

102

'Bracelets?' I said. 'Where the hell did you get 'em?'

'Borrowed off Willy,' he said.

'You think of everything, don't you, Charlie?'

'You better believe it,' he said.

Dorf was becoming *compos mentis*. When I groped for his hand, he began to struggle away from me. I was tempted to use my fist, but held back from hurting the poor sad bugger. He had been abused quite enough. I always hated the use of drugs, even when their use was employed as a necessary last resort. So I tried to subdue him without using violence, and as we thrashed around, Charlie said:

'Christ! What the hell are you playing at?'

'Just drive, Charlie,' I said, and when the cuffs were attached, 'where's the key?'

'No key.'

'Do you mean to tell me we don't have a key?'

'I'll keep the key,' he said. 'You just keep Sunshine.'

'Do I have any choice?'

'Ask yourself,' he said.

\*　　　\*　　　\*

The omniscient bastard was right, of course. With the handcuffs firmly secured, I felt free to drift into blessed oblivion. I didn't know how long Charlie drove, and had no idea where he finally stopped. I was vaguely aware of an absence of motion and must have opened my eyes and been briefly conscious of stillness and darkness, but the hard thing clamped on my wrist was not enough to stay me from slumber. I do not remember the sleep, but I vividly remember the waking. Every bone in my body felt sore, and those in my neck radiated agony. When I opened my eyes, I closed them again almost immediately against a pale dawn light which seemed as fierce as a desert sun. But my eyelids gave small relief, and there was pain in my wrist where the steel had chafed. Dorf was out to the world, snoring like a sow in pig. Charlie, in front, had his head laid back, and was breathing regularly. I doubted that he was still sleeping, but I pretended to be, because I knew that when I 'woke' we'd be up and away. A covert view all around told me we were

103

stashed in a lay-by secluded from a road somewhere between Frankfurt and Lübeck. A foul smell pervaded the car in spite of Charlie's wound-down window, but I tried to go back to sleep. My mouth was dry and my tongue tasted poisonous and I was sharply in need of a pee, and the stench from Dorf's clothes was sickening. But all of these things weighed as naught against my fervid wish for more rest.

'You awake?' Charlie said.

I hadn't moved, but I knew that he knew.

'No, I'm not,' I said. 'Where the hell are we?'

'Just short of Hamburg,' he said. So he'd driven the best part of two hundred miles.

'You can't have had any kip!'

'I've had enough. Get the laddo outside before he wets his pants.'

'Then what?'

'Then, we get on our way.'

I never felt less like driving, but, 'Right, one condition,' I said. 'This is where we swap places.'

'No need for that,' he said.

'I want to live long enough to get my breakfast.'

'Now look, Farrow—'

'Bollocks,' I said, and the way I said it drove daggers through my skull. 'We'll be in amongst traffic soon, and if you think I'm going to sit back here while you nod off at the wheel...'

He heaved a great sigh, and shook his head. 'Take Dorf out for a piss.'

'In a minute. How far to Hamburg?'

'Maybe thirty miles.'

I did a mental sum. Say fifty kilometres south of the city, another fifty further to go. Charlie had driven through most of the night. Suddenly, I felt ashamed. I felt like a passenger along for the ride. I *felt* his vast fatigue, and somehow the feeling imbued me with strength.

'Okay, let's have the key.'

The fact that he surrendered the key to the cuffs was oddly comforting. It represented a tacit admission of trust and reliance on me, just as I had always relied on him. It underlined the mutual faith which had always, in spite of our many differences, sustained the relationship. As I leaned across Dorf to open the car door, he said:

'Watch him, Farrow.'

'No sweat.'

Dorf came awake reluctantly. I pushed him out of the car, and he almost dragged me on top of him when he stumbled down on his knees. I hauled him upright, and linked together, we both had a much-needed pee. God preserve the inventor of zips, because buttons might have been too much for either of us to handle. Dorf was regaining his nouse. As he sprayed the weeds which fringed the lay-by, he sniffed at the air of new dawn, and cocked an ear to the burgeoning traffic.

'Where are you taking me?'

As I shook the drops off, 'We're taking you home.'

'Home? Where is "home"?' he said.

'If you don't know where home is, you must be unfortunate.'

'And you are so lucky,' he said. 'You are English—'

'British. And pull your zip up,' I said.

'English, British, what is the difference? You have homes,' he said. 'You can always retreat to your little island.'

'Fortunes of war,' I said.

'No. Fortunes of birth.'

'Well, whatever. Just behave yourself. Try to make trouble, you're going to regret it.'

He laughed. 'Regret?' he said. 'Those who are dead are beyond regret.'

'You're not dead yet,' I said.

'Are you saying that where there is life there is hope?'

'Something like that,' I said.

'A time to live, and a time to die?'

'Ecclesiastes,' I said, 'but never mind the philosophy. Zip yourself up, and let's go.'

'One moment. I think I am going to be sick.'

'Get on with it, then,' I said.

I had to be firm, even brutal, because four or five minutes had passed. Four or five minutes during which Charlie must surely have had his own pee—he performed his ablutions in the strictest of privacy—and would be expecting us back, even allowing for contingencies. The experience was mystical. That emptying of my bladder by the side of a scummy canal—the flow was too sluggish for any river—remains ensconced in my mind. Tiny details sometimes escape, but I would never seek to go back, because the memory is one I would rather forget. Nothing to do with the *place*, much more to do with the people. Or, person.

'Come on, Dorf,' I said. I let him gaze at the algae-slimed water for a further ten seconds or so, then jerked at the chain which bonded us. 'That's it. Time to go.'

'A time to live, and a time to die?'

He seemed resigned to his fate, but a sudden instinct promoted caution. The short sleep had done me some good, and when he swung his right fist at me, the training asserted itself. I sensed it coming and jerked away and his knuckles glanced off my skull instead of, probably, breaking my jaw. And a blow from his second-best fist was just no match against one from my best. I swung it round, very hard, and felt it smash on the side of his face. He collapsed with a strangled cry, and almost dragged me down with him. I staggered to stay on my feet, but was forced to stoop with my head bent low and as I struggled for breath, a voice at my back said:

'Finished now, are you?'

Dorf was sprawled in the weeds, the tallest stalks of which brushed my face. I heaved him up onto his arse, and turned my head to look at Charlie. He was looming over us, hands in his raincoat pockets.

'What kept you?'

'Nothing. I knew he couldn't get far, dragging *your* big fat carcase.'

'Jesus Christ!'

'Get up.'

Get up? I felt like lying down. I turned my head and saw, all along the fringe of the lay-by, a plethora of filthy junk. Rusting cans, empty cartons, and the ubiquitous plastic bags. Ugly evidence that man is vile.

'Give me a minute,' I said.

106

'You've already had a minute.'

'All right, *all right!*' I said. 'So give me another minute!'

'Balls. Get him unlocked,' Charlie said.

I was glad to take that thing off my wrist. 'There you go, he's all yours.' Charlie snapped the cuff on himself and used the toe of one shoe to nudge Dorf, very hard, in the ribs. 'Hey, come on Chas, take it easy!'

'Sod off. Start the car,' he said.

\*　　\*　　\*

The drive up to Lübeck passed with only one incident. No more than twenty minutes on, when I saw the sign for a Services stop, I veered into the access lane. A glance up into the rear-view mirror told me Charlie was asleep, but when I stopped the car in a slot on the carpark he woke up instantly and looked around and said:

'What's all this?'

'Refreshment, Charlie,' I said.

I half expected the usual argument, but he merely nodded his head. 'All right, but listen—'

'I know. Don't linger.'

Inside, no welcoming smell. I could have wolfed a plate of ham and eggs, but this was Germany, so I settled on half a dozen cheese rolls, two for each of us. I got the hot drinks from a machine in the lobby, disgorged into styrofoam cups. The coffee seemed decent, but the tea looked ghastly. Nothing to be done about that. Charlie would just have to like it, or lump it. I did a balancing act with the tray, and hurried outside to the BMW.

'About bloody time,' Charlie said. He unlocked the bracelet on his wrist so that Dorf could use both hands, and as I leaned over to pass them their scoff, 'All clear?' he said.

'Yes,' I said. 'All appears quiet on this western front.'

'Sure nothing stirring?'

'No.' A double negative, but what the hell.

'What's *this* supposed to be?'

'It's supposed to be tea.'

'It's supposed to be *what*?'

'When in Rome,' I said.

107

Dorf said nothing. He was too busy eating, tearing at the soft bread rolls between noisy gulps of coffee. I knew he was dumping it down to fill an empty aching void.

'Witch-piss!'

'Yes, I know, but sup it, Charlie. It's wet, and it's hot.'

'It's worse than witch-piss!'

'It was that, or nothing.'

'Bloody typical.'

'Look—what did you want me to do? Start complaining, draw attention?'

'Don't get smart.'

'God forbid.'

'You finished yet, are you?'

'Not hardly.'

I was starting on my second cheese roll as he was brushing the crumbs off his lap. Even Dorf wasn't yet done, and Dorf was really stashing it away. But Charlie took his left wrist, and snapped the cuff back onto it. Dorf tried weakly to resist.

*'Ein Moment, bitte!'*

'Bollocks,' Charlie said. 'Farrow, get going.'

'Christ! Can't I just finish?' My mouth was full of cheese roll. I gulped at the coffee in order to swallow, stuffed the rest of the roll in my mouth, and washed it down with the dregs from my cup. 'Take it easy!'

'No way. Ditch the rubbish, and get a move on.'

'What's all the panic?' I said.

'Never you mind.'

'For God's sake, Charlie, we're free and clear!'

'Are we hell as like,' he said.

So I ditched the rubbish and got back in the car and we hit the road again after a lapse of no more than fifteen minutes. We were now many miles beyond the turn-off for Brunswick, heading north instead of east and both 'friend' (Willy Schumacher) and 'foe' (the Cousins) were, hopefully, convinced that Dorf was being taken to Marienberg for transit to East Berlin, traditional venue for any exchange and quite the most logical place. But Charlie's great strength was a flouting of logic. He was never just one move ahead, he was rarely satisfied with fewer than several.

'Coming into Hamburg,' I said.

'Take the ring road up to Lübeck.'

'What then?'

'Wait and see.'

Our destination lay north-east of Hamburg at a distance of about forty miles. We had left the rain far behind, but were buffeted now by a rising wind. Gusts of it rocked the car, and tore at tarpaulin load-covers of the snarling juggernauts which jostled for position along the two nearside lanes. But I managed to make quite good time, and in a little more than half an hour we reached the autobahn exit sign. The clover-leaf dropped onto Fackenburger Allee and we rolled into town, with the big Hauptbahnhof over to our right. I began to recognise landmarks and soon it all came back.

Lübeck, once a Hanseatic republican state, is an ancient and very beautiful city. The original medieval settlement, now known as the Old Town, is built upon an island little more than a mile in width and half again as long, formed by the rivers Trave and Wakenitz. This natural fortress is surrounded on all sides by a sprawl of largely self-contained suburbs of which Travemünde, nine miles north, is easily the most widely known. Blankensee, five miles south, is where the wartime airfield was situated and where, in that terrible winter of 1945, I spent the coldest six months of my life.

As I negotiated the big traffic island at the end of the Holstentor Platz, Charlie said 'Take the Holstentorbrücke.'

So I slowed down to pass through the narrow arched gateway which seems to keep the massive round towers with their conical slate roofs from falling inwards upon each other, and we crossed a wind-whipped river over the narrow old bridge. The island citadel is traversed lengthways by two straight thoroughfares which run roughly parallel, and these are crossed at intervals by a network of narrow streets which fall east and west off the long low hog-back to the water on either side. Königsstrasse, widest of the two main streets, stretches from the centuries-old Burgtor Gate at the northern tip of the island, to the Muhlenbrücke in the south. As we came up to Königsstrasse:

109

'Start navigating, then,' I said.

'Turn right, and then take the third on the left.'

'You can't be serious,' I said. 'That's got to be Hundestrasse.'

'Congratulations,' he said.

'You're not going to tell me it's Fischer's house?'

'Fischer's been ten years dead. Lot of water under the bridge. Times change.'

'True,' I said, 'but Jesus, Charlie, *Fischer's* house!' [See *The Hamburg Switch*.]

'What's wrong with it?' he said.

'It was blown, for Christ's sake!'

'"Was" is correct. So just get on with it.'

My gut was assailed by a tremor of foreboding. I knew he was probably quite right. Edgar Allan Poe and *The Purloined Letter*. You want to hide something, stick it under the seeker's nose where it's sure to be overlooked. It was not that the seekers in that particular instance were likely to be seeking me still, but the place had gruesome associations and the thought of returning to it now was not a thought to inspire comfort.

'So whose was *this* bright idea?'

'Never mind whose idea it was—and watch that lorry!' he said.

Lübeck is even worse than Ripon in the matter of tortuous streets which never were meant for motor vehicles. 'Old' is picturesque, but it isn't conducive to modern transport. The grandeur of centuries long gone is lost on the driver of a motor car. The burghers of Lübeck were given a heaven-sent opportunity—absolutely no pun—to rebuild their town after a bombing devastation, courtesy of the RAF, during the Easter devotions of 1942. They could have started from scratch. Instead, they went to ancient archives and rebuilt the city as it was in the twelfth and thirteenth centuries, narrow cobbled streets and all. They sifted the rubble and used the material to re-create their town, and the resurrected buildings—especially the Königstrasse church—still emanate an atmosphere of times long gone.

As I turned into Hundestrasse, 'There's a garage, now,' Charlie said. 'Underneath, on the other side.'

'A garage? No way!' I said. 'There's not enough room to turn into a garage.'

'Yes, there is. Just slow down.'

'I'm telling you, Charlie, it's too damned tight to get this big bugger in!'

'Well, get your fat arse out of it and open the door,' he said, 'and I'll put the bloody thing in myself.'

'Don't get excited,' I said.

'Excited? Jesus! Go on, get it open!'

The up-and-over door was so well oiled it raised itself. I heard the motor growl, and stood well back to let him drive in. The cobbled street was so narrow it barely allowed the passage of a car, much less the manoeuvre necessary to make a right-angle turn. Even Charlie couldn't make it without a harsh scrape of one wing, and as he ducked out of the BMW:

'See? I told you,' I said.

'You told me nothing. Shut the door.'

The car's nearside was barely three inches away from the garage wall, forcing egress from offside. Charlie eased out, dragging Dorf after him. When the door rolled down, the garage, at half past eight in the morning, was suddenly dark as a cave. A voice in the blackness said:

'Switch on the lintel, half-way up left-hand side.'

I groped for the switch, and found it and pressed it, and immediately closed my eyes against the brilliant flickering of a neon tube. When I opened them again, the garage was flooded with hard white light.

'Can we relax, now?' I said.

'Don't talk wet. Get the bags out.'

'I knew you'd say that,' I said.

*       *       *

The interior of the house was exactly as I remembered it. Except, of course, that it now had a garage. Subsequent occupants had sacrificed precious living room in favour of a mere machine. *Vanitas vanitatum, et omnia vanitas.* What fools we mortals are. A door gave access to the space left for people, and Charlie motioned me through. I entered with

111

Charlie close behind me, pulling Dorf in tow, and found myself in that long narrow passage with stairs climbing off to the left but now, aside from the little kitchen, only one other room on the ground. As I turned into it I recognised the carpet, and furnishings. The only alien note was struck by the person perched on one of the armchairs, smoking a small cigar. That person was waiting for us to enter.

'Well hello there, Edna,' I said. 'Don't get up.'

'I have no intention. So you made it, Charles,' she said.

'What's it look like?' Same old Charlie. He dragged Dorf into the room, thrust him down into one of the chairs, and took the handcuffs off. Dorf just slumped there, massaging his wrist. 'Quiet, Edna?'

'As the grave. It seems they're watching Marienberg.'

'Who's "they"?'

'The Cousins, and Willy Schumacher's boys.'

'Good. Let 'em watch,' Charlie said.

Edna's girlish giggle belied her obvious age. 'I'm afraid they're going to be awfully upset.' She mashed out the stub of her cigar. 'So you got my message.'

'What message?' I said.

The question was ignored. Edna got to her feet. 'Do you want some breakfast?'

'Not half!'

Ignored again. Charlie shook his head. 'No, thanks. We've had it,' he said.

'A cheese roll is not a breakfast, Charlie.'

'*Two* cheese rolls,' he said.

Edna grinned. She was enjoying the exchange. As we took our raincoats off, she looked from one to the other of us.

'There's a difference of opinion here.'

'That's right,' I said, 'so what are you offering?'

'Bacon and eggs?'

'Sounds great.'

'What about you, Charlie?'

'Jesus!'

'Could you do him a pot of *real* tea?'

'Certainly. Indian, or China?'

'There you go, Chas,' I said. 'What more could you ask?'

'Exactly. Sit down and relax,' Edna said.

She had risen to her feet without pushing herself up—not bad for such an old bird—using both hands to smooth her short grey hair. She was wearing a real tartan kilt with a beige cashmere twin-set and neat short-heeled shoes whose glow, by the look of them, derived from years of fond polishings. Woollen stockings on still-shapely legs, and the whole straight out of *Country Life*.

'Listen, Edna,' I said, 'I wouldn't want to put you to any trouble . . .'

'No trouble at all,' she said.

When she left the room, Charlie said 'Watch the boyo.'

'Why? Where are you going?' I said.

'Never mind where I'm going. Just watch him.'

'Better leave me the gun, then,' I said.

'Gun? What gun?'

'The one in your pocket, the U.S. Army Colt's,' I said. 'The one you took off Kramer.'

'You're imagining things,' he said. 'And in any case, guns make loud noises. Think of the neighbours.'

'So what?'

'Are you trying to tell me you can't handle him?'

'Normally, no problem,' I said, 'but I happen to be knackered.'

'So is Sunshine, so that makes you even,' he said. He paused at the door. 'Get a grip on yourself.'

'Oh, bugger off Charlie,' I said.

So he buggered off and left me with Dorf who seemed, sagged deep in his chair, incapable of mischief and resigned to his fate. I had no wish to talk to him, and so the room fell silent. I had heard Charlie mount the stairs, probably to run a check on the bathroom, and that Edna was busy in the kitchen was obvious by the redolent air. The homely odours induced relaxation and my nagging fears became lulled by a wishful reach for normality. There was no noise of traffic, not even pedestrian, up or down the street outside, and only faint stirrings within the house. The loudest sound I could hear was the gentle rhythm of my own deep breathing.

But *'watch him'* Charlie had said, and I must admit to

having failed. All three of us were fagged out, but desperation lends superhuman strength. I woke with Dorf's hands on my throat, and reacted purely by instinct. He had made the venial mistake of straddling my thighs as he bent over me, and when my knee hit his groin he took its full force on an unprotected scrotum. Then, as his head came down, I butted him hard with the crown of my skull and smashed the bridge of his nose and his hands lost their grip and he fell back off me. He sprawled down flat on his back on the rug in front of the fireplace, with blood gushing over his face. I was still leaning forward with elbows on knees, sucking in huge draughts of breath, when a voice from the doorway said:

'Bravo.'

'And up yours, Charlie,' I gasped.

'I *told* you to watch him.'

'All right, so I watched him.'

'Like hell you did,' Charlie said. 'It's lucky I got here.'

'Bullshit.'

'What's happening?' Edna said.

She had appeared in the doorway beside Charlie, clutching a spatula, a plastic apron protecting her clothes against splashes from the frying pan.

Charlie said, 'It's nothing, Edna.' Then, to me, 'Get him up.'

'Right. Come on, then, give us a hand.'

'A hand, my arse!' he said. He tossed me the handcuffs' key. 'Left wrist to right ankle.'

'Hey, come on!'

'Is that necessary, Charles?' Edna said.

'It is with this daft bugger.'

'All right, don't rub it in.'

I was linking Dorf's left wrist to his ankle.

'Let him get out of *that*,' Charlie said.

I straightened up. 'He's in a bad way.'

'He's not so bad,' Charlie said, 'as not to be able to have a go.'

'I managed him, didn't I?' I said. 'So now get on with your knitting.'

'The knitting's all done,' Charlie said. Then, 'You finished

114

out there, Edna?'

'Just the eggs,' Edna said. 'Give me another three minutes.'

She turned and moved out of sight, leaving Charlie alone in the doorway. He looked down, derisorily, at Dorf, who was grunting and snorting out blood and snot, mumbling unintelligibly. In a way, I felt sorry for him. Feelings are often confused. That part of my mind which felt pity was besieged by a sense of disgust, and even less worthy, a tinge of disdain. Who shall cast the first stone? Disdain is a cheap and invidious concept because it allows many forms, few of which bear close scrutiny.

'Breakfast, boys!' Edna called.

Dorf was beyond eating breakfast. He was curled on his side on the rug with his left wrist secured to the opposite ankle.

'I've broken his nose,' I said. 'He should see a doctor.'

'Tough.'

'I'm telling you Charlie, he needs a doctor.'

'Listen,' Charlie said, 'you asked for some breakfast, so eat it.'

'What about you?' I said.

'I'm going for a bath. You stuff yourself, but *this* time, *watch* him—okay?'

That breakfast, prepared and served by Edna on a tray which I balanced on my knees, tasted better than any I'd ever eaten. Nothing special about the food—it was, after all, only bacon and eggs—but the rolls were fresh and good and the unsalted butter was delicious. So, too, was the tea, and tired as I was, I made a pig of myself. Edna smoked and watched as I ate, enjoying my pleasure vicariously. Dorf stayed coiled on the rug. There came from upstairs a gurgling of water pipes, Charlie having finished his bath. I used a chunk of bread to mop yolk off my plate, slurped on my second mug of tea, and said to Edna:

'Beautiful.'

'I'm glad you enjoyed it,' she said. 'But see here, Farrow, I'm worried about Charles.'

'You and me both,' I said.

'Listen, I'm serious.'

'So am I.'

'He's older than you think.'

'He's as old as the rest of us, as old as he feels.'

'He's not taking care of himself.'

'It's no good trying to tell him anything. I've known him for twenty-five years.'

'Charles and I have been friends for almost forty.'

'All right, Edna,' I said, 'so when you were kids you played doctors and nurses, but me and that awkward old sod have seen each other through some pretty rough times.'

'Do you think I don't know that?' she said.

'I wouldn't be surprised at what you know.'

'Yes, you would,' Edna said. 'I know as much about you two as probably you know yourselves.'

'Well, in that case, you'll know that this is our last one.'

'It's the last one for me, too,' she said. 'And it's going to be the last for a great many others.'

'Leave off, Edna,' I said. 'The Section isn't all *that* big.'

'I'm not only talking about the Section, Farrow, I'm talking about the whole shebang. Don't you read the newspapers?'

'Only the book reviews.'

'They're going to dismantle the Berlin Wall.'

'That'll be the day.'

'Mark my words. It'll be gone within a year.'

'I hope you're right,' I said.

She changed the subject. 'You've been here before—here in this house, I mean.'

'Have I?'

'When you and young McKenzie pulled off the Hamburg switch.'

'I don't remember.'

'Fiddlesticks! Who do you suppose helped set it up?'

'Any more tea in your teapot?'

She laughed, and stubbed out her small cigar. 'You and Charles are two of a kind.'

'Hey, I thought you liked me!' I said.

'Give me your tray, and I'll make some more tea.'

'No, don't bother,' I said. 'I just thought there might be some left in the pot. Really, I've had enough.'

116

Edna removed my tray, and when she returned she did not sit down again. She stood, arms folded, just inside the door, looking down at Dorf.

'How long does Charles intend to leave him like that?'

'Don't ask me,' I said.

'He'll be in a better mood when he's bathed and shaved.'

'Now I *know* that you know him,' I said. 'By the way, what about sleeping arrangements?'

'Same as when you were here before. Upstairs hasn't altered, there are still just two bedrooms—oh, I see what you mean! No, I shan't be staying. You can have separate rooms.'

'Thank God for that,' I said.

'Why? Does Charles snore?'

'Well, one of us does.'

She gave vent to her merry laugh and Charlie, who had appeared at her back, said:

'What's going on? What's the joke?'

I was relieved to see that he was contemplating sleep. Tootal dressing gown, Marks & Spencer's pyjamas, slippers on his feet.

'I was just telling Edna the one about the milkman.'

'What milkman? Sober up!'

'Chance would be a fine thing, Charlie.'

'Yes, well get yourself scrubbed,' he said. 'You smell like a Burmese . . .'

'Burmese what?'

'Brothel?' Edna said.

I was growing quite attached to Edna. She really was some jolly old lass. Charlie, however, was not amused. Nor, it seemed, was Dorf. He lay with eyes closed and gave no sign of having heard any of this. Charlie glanced down at him, and then up at me.

'Right, then.'

'I'm on my way. Do I take it I can roll straight into bed?'

'Yes, you might as well. Get some kip, you're going to need it.'

'I knew there'd be a snag,' I said.

There wasn't a lot of hot water left, but I had a lukewarm bath and felt all the better for it. I had lugged our bags upstairs, but now only mine remained on the landing. Charlie had chosen the room in which McKenzie and I had found Fischer and that, by me, was fine. It reduced the chances of my being haunted by his ghost. The room he had left to me was smaller of the two, but I couldn't have cared less. I rolled naked into the bed, and fell at once into blessed oblivion. The time was around ten a.m.

*       *       *

'Farrow, wake up. Come on, rise and shine. I've brought you a cup of tea.'

The voice which dredged me out of my dreams was that of Edna.

'*Wha*—?'

'I said, I've brought you a cup of tea.'

'Jesus!'

'No, only me.'

'Edna, you're an angel. What time is it?'

'Half past three.'

'Afternoon or morning? Where's Charlie?'

'Downstairs, and he's waiting for you.'

'Let him wait.'

'D'you want me to tell him that? Come on, boy, you'd better get up.' As I pushed myself up against the pillows, the bedclothes fell down about my waist, and Edna said: 'My goodness, you *have* been in the wars!'

I pulled up the sheet to cover the embroidery. 'You should see the other guys,' I said, and as I took the steaming mug from her hand. 'How's Dorf?'

'We've cleaned him up, and he's eaten something, and he's not so bad.'

'I wouldn't want to trade damaged goods.'

'Nonsense!' No humour in Edna now. Her manner was tough as cold steel. 'Who cares, so long as you can swap him for Hector?'

'So it's *Hector*, is it?' I said. 'Don't tell me he's a relative of *yours*, as well!'

'As well as what?'

'As well as—sorry, forget it. Tell the boss-man I'll be right

118

down.'

'I wouldn't procrastinate if I were you.'

'That's a fancy word, Edna,' I said.

I drank the tea as I donned my clothes. My last set of clean underwear, and my last pair of socks, and my last clean shirt. Someone—it had to be Edna—had sponged and pressed my suit, but my shoes were still spattered by spots of Dorf's vomit. I used wadded toilet roll to clean off the muck, flushed the wads down the loo, and went downstairs feeling smart and dapper.

'Beau Brummel, at last,' Charlie said.

He was sitting in one of the armchairs which flanked the fireplace, with Edna sitting opposite. They had moved Dorf onto the couch, and now he was cuffed at wrists only. The blood had been washed off his face, but the flesh around his eyes was swollen and discoloured, a study in purple and green. He slumped there, epitome of misery, staring dully at his knees.

'Had much trouble with him, have you, Charlie?'

'Don't get snotty,' he said. 'Sit yourself down, and listen.'

'What about old Sunshine here?'

'I don't give a monkey's whether he listens or not.'

'All right, I'm all ears,' I said.

Charlie appeared to be back on top form, in control of all he surveyed. He might have stepped out of a Burton's shop window. As he rearranged his clothes, he made me feel positively scruffy. I fingered the knot of my tie, patted my breast-pocket handkerchief, and ran a quick check on the shoes. After all these years, he still had that effect. Edna was enjoying the show. Her bright button eyes followed every nuance.

'All right if *I* stay, Charles?' she said.

Charlie looked at his wrist watch. 'When's the latest you have to leave?' As if he didn't already know.

'Four-thirty, five o'clock.'

'No great rush, then.'

'That's right,' I said, 'so what about us having a jar?'

'Forget it, Farrow!'

'Why not?' said Edna, and I warmed to her even more. 'Farrow, name your poison.'

119

'You got any whisky?' I said.

'Only malt, only Glenmorangie.'

'*Only?* Good heavens!' I said. 'Marry me, Edna.'

'Not likely. I want to be wanted for myself.'

Charlie, of course, was hating all this. 'Now look, you two' he said, 'cut the bloody comedy.'

'No comedy, Charles,' Edna said, 'we are merely observing the social graces.'

'Edna—!' Charlie said.

She paused at the door with a smile full of innocence. 'Yes, Charles?'

'Just watch it,' he said.

She flashed me a wink as she left the room, and, 'That's a great little lady,' I said. 'You're lucky to have such an understanding friend.'

'Listen, pillock,' he said, 'you just keep your mind on the job!'

'Don't tell me you're jealous,' I said.

'Jealous? What the *hell* are you talking about?'

'It's an ugly emotion,' I said. 'It's unworthy of you, old buddy.'

'Don't give me that "old buddy" shit. I'm warning you, Farrow—'

'Warning him of what?' Edna was back with the drinks. One for herself, and one for me. 'Are you sure you won't have something, Charles?'

'How many more times do I have to tell you?'

'Edna, cheers,' I said.

'To your good health, Farrow.'

'And to yours. *Sláinte!*'

'Bottoms up.'

Ours might be seen as a childish performance, but dichotomise the man from the child and you sever the link between hope eternal and harsh reality and that, in a business such as ours, is a morbid prospect indeed. So Edna and I celebrated rapport by imbibing that most excellent of malts whilst Charlie fumed and Dorf sat quiescent.

Stillness in the eye of a storm.

\*     \*     \*     ˬ

120

Edna left the house at about five o'clock. I had no idea, at the time, where she might have been going. It might have been back to Berlin, or it could have been into a house down the street, or to one of the hotels in town. All I know for sure is that she walked away, because she couldn't have parked a car anywhere within about four hundred metres.

'What now, Charlie?' I said.

He adjusted, again, the creases in his trousers, smoothed the tight little waves of his hair, and settled back and said:

'We wait.'

'How long?'

'As long as it takes.'

'You sound like Arthur Scargill.'

'Who the hell's Arthur Scargill?' he said.

I knew that he knew perfectly well who Arthur Scargill was. It was just his inimitable way of expressing derision, and dismissal.

'So what's on the menu?' I said. 'Or are we all dressed up with nowhere to go?'

'Don't you believe it,' he said.

'I trust the action will not become physical?'

'You sound like Gary Lineker,' he said. Charlie never ceased to amaze with the vast parameters of his esoteric knowledge.

'This isn't a game of soccer,' I said. 'Football', in Yorkshire, means Rugby League.

'Just bear that in mind, then,' he said. 'Anyway, why should you worry? You've filled your big fat gut, and you've had a good kip—what more do you want?'

'I want to go home,' I said. 'I want to go home, and see my old dog.'

'Don't start that again. We're all going home.'

'When?'

'Tomorrow.'

'You know what they say, Chas. Tomorrow never comes.'

'Bullshit. We make our own tomorrows.'

'So tell me how, then,' I said. 'Tell me how we make this particular tomorrow.'

'Piece of cake,' Charlie said. 'We swap old Sunshine—' he looked sideways at Dorf '—for young McKenzie.'

'How?'

'Don't worry about the details.'

'Listen, Charlie,' I said, 'I'm committed for various reasons, to getting young Jock back home but I want to know, *right now*, what's involved!'

'You're not going to like it,' he said.

\* \* \*

He was right. I didn't like it. But, and try as I might, I could not think of a better way.

'It's too bloody risky,' I said.

'Risky, my arse. It's a piece of piss.'

We had talked in front of Dorf because, at this stage, it mattered little whether he heard us or not. He was nothing more than a joint of meat for sale on a butcher's slab. The analogy disturbed me, but did not deter me. Solomon, pack your bags.

'Charlie, I'm having another drink.'

'All right, just one more,' he said.

The tiny kitchen was immaculate, the dishes all clean and stacked, and Edna had left us a pile of sandwiches. Just imagine that. A lady of quality washing up after *me*, Marcus Aurelius Farrow, thrice lucky to be alive and with never much more than a pot to pee in. This whimsical thought charged my mind as I looked into cupboards in search of the bottle and found it on the top left-hand side. I added water from the tap, tested for strength and taste, and sloshed in more whisky just for good measure. Nothing would have comforted me more than to make myself gently, peacefully drunk. A prospect much to be wished, but one which I knew was a definite non-starter.

Charlie looked first to my glass, then at the sandwiches, and then at my face. 'Happy now, are you?' he said. 'I hardly need tell you—'

'In that case, why bother?'

'—you've a busy night ahead.'

122

*　　*　　*

I thought we might have taken the cuffs off our guest and maybe have given him a jar, but Charlie vetoed both suggestions so Dorf ate his scoff with both hands, like some enormous squirrel. I washed mine down with malt, the other two with mugs of tea. Good enough for Charlie, good enough for Dorf. I brushed stray crumbs off my knees.

'I wonder where Edna got that beautiful boiled ham?'

'What's it matter?' Charlie said.

'Not a lot. I only wondered.'

'Jesus, Farrow,' he said, 'is that all you ever think about?'

'That, and the Other,' I said.

'The other what?'

'Oh, Gawd!'

'You talk like a village idiot.'

'*Ship's* idiot, if you don't mind.' I broke the inevitable silence which followed by asking, 'All right then, what now?'

'We're waiting for Edna.'

'So she's coming back, is she?'

'If she wasn't,' Charlie said, 'we wouldn't be waiting for her, would we?'

'The question was rhetorical,' I said.

'What's "rhetorical"?'

'Come off it!'

'So talk a bit of sense,' Charlie said.

'All right, a straight question: what's she up to?'

'She's hiring us a boat.'

'A boat? Why the hell do we need a boat?'

'To make the swap, of course.'

'Oh, no! Don't tell me!'

'What's the problem? Nobody's going to get wet.'

'Nobody?'

'Nobody.'

'That's all right, then. Last time, I damn nearly drowned.'

'That was last time. This time, *I'm* here.'

'Sure. Big deal,' I said.

'Anyway, you're the naval expert.'

123

'That depends what you have in mind.'

'The Man's relying on us, Farrow.'

'Bugger the Man,' I said.

'Listen, one more crack like that, I'll kick the shit out of you!'

I wouldn't have put it past him, and should he try, he might well succeed. I wasn't prepared to run that risk, so:

'Okay, Tiger,' I said, 'what's the score?'

'Are you listening, now?'

'Yes, I'm listening,' I said.

*      *      *

Dorf voiced his need to attend a call of nature.

'Take him up, Farrow.'

'Why me?'

'Because I say so, and I'm the boss.'

'So *that's* why I get the nice jobs.'

'Here's the key, and watch him. Don't take your eyes off the sod.'

'He can't run far with his britches round his ankles—come on then, Dorf,' I said.

I made him leave the lavatory door wide open and leaned against the landing wall and watched him at his occasions. Not an inspiring sight. I wouldn't take a job nursing geriatrics for half of all the money in the world. The prospect of having to do this for a *living* . . .

'Hurry up, Dorf,' I said.

'I cannot do it with somebody watching.'

'Well, pretend I'm not here,' I said.

He finally completed his toilet, and I snapped the cuffs back on.

'How am I to wash my hands?'

'Wash 'em as best you can.'

'I would also like to have a shave.'

'We love you just as you are, whiskers and all.'

'You think my plight amusing!'

'Hilarious,' I said.

'You know you will never complete this business?'

'That's what they all say,' I said.

124

'The Russkis will shoot me, and keep their exchange man.'

'They wouldn't dare,' I said, 'because that would upset my partner, and when my partner gets upset, the consequences are most disconcerting.'

'This is not a joke, my friend.'

'I'm not your friend, so get a move on.'

I affected indifference to his chat, but truth to tell, it raised doubts in my mind. I would have preferred to make the swap on dry land, because *terra firma* is immutable and predictable. So far as I was aware, there had never been an exchange at sea.

'*What's going on up there?*'

'We're coming down now, keep your hair on!' Then, 'Right, you go first, Dorf,' I said.

'I was beginning to think he'd done you an injury.'

'Bollocks, Charlie,' I said. I prodded Dorf back to his seat on the sofa. 'The laddo's been telling me that he thinks the Others will try to pull a fast one.'

'He could be right,' Charlie said.

'Are you saying, now, that there might be more aggro?'

'What d'you mean, *more*?' he said. 'All you've done so far is stuff your guts and get your head down.'

'Okay. My fault for believing your rhubarb about this one being a piece of cake.'

'A piece of cake is just what it is.'

'So far, perhaps,' I said, 'but I don't feel easy about the rest of it, matey.'

'Farrow, you worry too much.'

'That's because I've got damn good cause.'

'You're a worrier.'

'Too bloody true!'

'Give over, for Christ's sake.'

'Knackers!'

Charlie appeared quite relaxed, but a tiny sound somewhere out in the hallway coincided with the fact that he suddenly had a gun in his fist, and when she appeared at the door its muzzle was pointing straight at her chest.

'Welcome home, Edna,' I said.

Her gaze roved from Charlie across to Dorf, and then she

winked at me as she tugged at the fingers of her dark green kid gloves.

'I see you're all comfy. How sweet.'

'Edna, let me take your coat.'

'Thank you, Farrow,' she said.

It was obvious from her change of clothing that she had to have a base not far from the house in Hundestrasse. Her voluminous tweed coat was so wondrously soft it might have been fashioned from the fleece of newborn lambs. She had changed her cashmere twin-set for another of a different hue to match the box-pleated skirt she now wore, with dark green shoes to complete the ensemble. Only the pearls looked the same. She composed herself at the end of the sofa on which our guest was crouched, and settled her handbag on her lap. What a fabulous old girl. She might have been attending a sedate family gathering.

'Sorry I'm late, Charles,' she said, 'but it took rather longer than anticipated.'

'What took longer?' I said.

Charlie said, 'Farrow, take Dorf upstairs.'

'No way, old buddy,' I said. 'I want to know what took longer than anticipated.'

'Yes, Charles, I think he should.'

'*Edna!*'

'*Mister* McGowan?'

She was the only person I ever knew who actually beat Charlie in a staring match.

'All right, smart-arse,' he said, 'get this geezer upstairs, and make certain he's secure.'

'Any suggestions as to how I do it?'

'Jesus, use your loaf!'

'There's a solid iron pipe in the airing cupboard.'

'Thank you, Edna,' I said. 'Come on, then, Sunshine, upsadaisy.'

'And you better tie his feet.'

I pushed Dorf ahead of me up the stairs and opened the airing-cupboard door. The slatted shelves above the cistern were piled with towels and sheets and neatly-ironed pillowcases. The big copper tank was well lagged, and the old iron pipe connected to it was bracketed on the skirting board with barely an inch of clearance, just about enough to allow for the cuff to be locked around it. But the available floor space was small, so that when I shackled Dorf to the pipe he had to lie half-in, half-out, with his trunk in the cupboard and his legs on the landing. I fetched him a pillow from my bed, and he thanked me mutely with eyes as soulful as those of my faithful old dog. Conscience stabbed like a knife in the ribs but then, by an effort of will, I made myself think of McKenzie.

'It's your own bloody fault, Dorf,' I said.

What I meant, of course, was that it wasn't *my* fault. Thus do we excuse ourselves for actions of which, deep-down, we're ashamed.

I could hear the faint murmur of voices, and I hurried back downstairs, anxious not to miss anything. As I made to close the sitting-room door, Charlie said:

'Leave it open, and listen.'

'He's not going anywhere,' I said, 'without he takes all the plumbing with him.'

'I can vouch for that,' Edna said, 'this old house is built like a fortress.'

'Satisfied, Charlie?' I said.

He paid no heed. 'Go on, then, Edna, tell him about the boat.'

She was setting fire to one of her cigars. As she stowed her lighter away, she said 'It's a nine-metre cabin cruiser—'

'Petrol engine?'

'What's the odds? Don't interrupt her, Farrow.'

'Look, I'm the naval expert. You said so yourself, did you not?'

'So what's the odds?'

'The odds are considerable, and I want to know from the start whether we're dealing with petrol, or diesel.'

'What difference does it make?'

'Petrol's more reliable. It's a damn sight more volatile, which means it's quicker off the mark. And if you don't think *that* might make a difference—'

'All right, all right, don't bang on. Edna—?'

'Petrol.'

'Inboard, or outboard?'

'Inboard. Two-hundred litre tank, and there's a couple of five-gallon jerrycans on board.'

'Jesus, Edna!' I said. 'Where are we making this swap— the North Cape?'

'We'll come to that later,' she said.

'So what sort of craft will the Others be using?'

'Now that we just don't know.'

'Come on!' I said. 'A whaler? A frigate? A bloody battleship?'

'You're getting hysterical, Farrow.'

'Damn right I am,' I said. *'Unidentified cabin cruiser rammed and lost without trace . . .* how does that little news item grab you?'

'For Christ's sake relax,' Charlie said. 'The terms call for no more than three on each ship.'

'Boat.'

'All right, pillock, *boat*. On ours, just you and me and Edna—'

'We are not taking Edna,' I said.

'That is not for you to decide.'

'Isn't it?' I said. 'So where can you get another skipper?'

'Are you two quite finished?' Edna said.

'Not by a long chalk. Listen, Charlie—'

'Any more from you,' he said, 'and I'll kick your arse back to where you came from.'

'Just make that a promise!' I said.

Edna killed the stub of her cigar, and 'Boys! Boys! Cool it!' she said. 'Save your energies for tomorrow morning.'

'So it's tomorrow, is it?' I said. 'Nobody tells me anything. I thought it was going to be tonight.'

'Really, Farrow. Not in darkness.'

'Well, that's one good thing, Edna,' I said, 'but I still don't want you with us.'

'We'll discuss that later,' she said. 'And now if you'll excuse me, I must go and powder my nose.'

'Check on Dorf while you're at it.'

'Naturally, Charles,' Edna said, and if he caught the irony in her tone he gave no sign of it. She gathered her gear about her in the manner of a ship leaving port, and when she was gone I said:

128

'Jesus, Charlie, you can't be serious about taking that lady along?'

As he rearranged his clothes, he sighed and said: 'I've no option, have I?'

'But you're supposed to be the boss-man,' I said.

'Your boss, yes, but I'm not Edna's boss. Edna gets her orders from the Man.'

'So where the hell does that leave me?'

'Same place as always,' he said. 'I tell you what to do, and you do it.'

'Yeah, well, sometimes,' I said, but I knew it would be capricious to argue because whenever events became fraught, his directives were always fast and incisive.

There came from somewhere above the sound of a lavatory flushing, and after a small lapse of time Edna rejoined us in the sitting room.

'You're very quiet,' she said.

'Farrow's thinking. Mark it in your diary.'

'Up yours, Charlie,' I said.

Edna chuckled and fished in her handbag for one of her thin cheroots. 'Mr Dorf appears to be sleeping.'

'Lucky old bugger,' I said.

Charlie said 'Watch your language, Farrow!'

'Oh, that's all right,' Edna said. 'I've heard much worse in my lifetime.'

'Not the point,' Charlie said.

Edna blew smoke towards the ceiling. 'So let us *get* to the point. I think that you, Farrow, should check the boat— though I'm sure you'll find it's okay.'

'Where's it moored?'

'Up in Travemünde.'

'Well, that figures,' I said.

And so it did, because at Travemünde all that separated East from West was the kilometre-wide channel at the mouth of the Trave, where it entered the Lübecker Bucht. But their half of the channel was heavily mined, as I knew to my erstwhile cost, so the swap would probably be made offshore. Not easy in such a small boat, but feasible given half-decent weather. I only hoped and prayed that the Cousins were still watching Marienberg, and the

129

Friedrichstrasse checkpoint in Berlin. 'How do I get up there?'

'Take the car.'

'Take the car, Charlie?' I said. 'I can't even get it out of the garage!'

'God Almighty!' he said. 'You need a bloody nursemaid!'

'Come on, boys,' Edna said, 'do stop being so fucking childish.' Then, as we both gaped at her, 'You, Charles, get the car out and you, Farrow, please close your mouth.'

When Charlie had gone to effect the manoeuvre, 'Edna, I'm shocked,' I said.

'Why?'

'That word . . .'

'Oh fiddle-de-dee, you must have heard it thousands of times during all those years in the Navy.'

'Yes, I know,' I said, 'but coming from a lady—'

'Don't be such a male chauvinist,' she said. 'Do you think we women are a different species?'

'Well . . . no.'

'There you go, then,' she said, and abruptly changed the subject. 'Now, I want you to go over this boat and make perfectly sure it will serve our purpose.'

'Before I can do that,' I said, 'I need to know what the purpose is.'

'Fair enough,' Edna said. She brushed cigar ash off her skirt, took another deep pull at the weed, and set it down in an ashtray balanced on the arm of the couch. 'We don't yet know the exact co-ordinates, but I'm guessing they'll want to rendezvous about twenty miles north of Travemünde.'

'The Baltic can be rough,' I said, 'too bloody rough for a couple of small boats to heave-to and come alongside.'

'Agreed, and already considered. So it's life-jackets,' Edna said, 'for both Dorf and Hector.'

'Very dicey,' I said. 'If it comes to that, we could be in trouble.'

'Farrow, it's up to us to cope with any such trouble.'

'All well and good,' I said, 'but you don't understand—'

'I *do* understand. All I want to know is whether or not you're on for the job. If not, now's the time to say no, and I for one wouldn't blame you.'

'First, I need to look at the boat.'
'Of course you do. And if you like it?'
'Full steam ahead,' I said.

*     *     *

I drove away from the house in Lübeck around about nine o'clock. The road up to Travemünde was quiet, very few private cars and even fewer commercial vehicles. I kept to a steady speed well within the legal limit. I needed time to think. Edna had given me the key to the boat and had told me where it was berthed. I stashed the BMW in the carpark of the Maritim Hotel, went inside and had a drink, then strolled along the waterfront. Very little had changed from last time, because the environment did not allow for much change. The odd scrap of litter now underfoot, but that was just a sign of the times, evidence of deteriorating standards common all over the world. The night was crisp and invigorating, with an infinite starry sky presaging fine weather on the morrow. The sea smelled beautifully clean but that, I knew, was a fond illusion. Yet, the old familiar tang of ozone brought back my sea-going days—*à la recherche du temps perdu*. Recollections quickly dispelled by impinging memories of a time much more recent and much less pleasant. Like in 1979 when McKenzie, just a brash raw kid still wet behind the ears, had rescued me from the deep and dirty. How could I, now, let him down? The old invidious *noblesse oblige*.

I knew I must have passed the boat, but I wasn't concerned about that. I walked all the way to the end of the Strand, then on to the tip of the point, and scanned the dark beach, with my hands in my pockets. So far as I could see, I was the only living creature in the whole wide world. Everyone else was indoors, sloshing down the gargle and chomping on the scoff. Travemünde was that sort of place. Most of its residents seemed to live in a sybaritic dream, one long Bacchanalia. Just across the water, life was much different. No happy laughing throng over there, just a wide sweep of beach stretching empty and desolate, heavily sown with mines and studded at intervals by ugly watch-towers. A string of buoys in the channel blinked their warning lights: venture so far, but no further, this is the Great Divide.

I suppressed an involuntary shudder, took one last long look out to sea, and turned about to retrace my steps. I felt most ineffably sad, like a man approaching the end of an era. I seemed to have outlived all the virtues which once were self-evident. My broodings were those of a man finally confronted with the onset of age.

That long stretch of the waterfront bastioned to provide berths for boats seemed exactly as I remembered it, flanked on the one side by leisure establishments, hotels and restaurants, and on the other by flotillas of boats moored in serried ranks, their fenders caressing the floating pontoons as they wallowed on the swell. Edna had told me that the *Kleine Olga* was lying alongside the wall near enough opposite a bierkeller called *Der Öststrand Hof*. When at last I spotted her, she came as a comforting surprise. She looked strong and sleek and seaworthy, and my faith in Edna was restored. So much to be said for outward appearance. I walked on past the boat, and when I was sure that nobody was paying attention to me, I retraced my route and took to the steps which descended to the pontoon from which I could step over *Olga*'s low side-rail. Her stern dipped under my weight, and I almost fell headlong down into the well-deck. Once I found firm footing I paused to turn around and make a sweep of the whole of the waterfront. Nothing, nothing at all. Not one single soul in sight. It was always possible, of course, that there could be a watcher behind some dark window, but I didn't think it likely. No. Edna would have been much too careful, there always comes a time when there's naught else to do but to trust somebody and should that trust prove misplaced, that's the time you're destined to pass beyond worry.

It quickly became obvious, and without any need for a survey, that the *Olga* was a very fine boat. She was beautifully fitted out, and no owner spends that much time and money without first being very sure that the hull is worth his effort. I shrank from imagining the cost of her hire, even for only one day. I would have loved to have owned such a cruiser. She was absolutely grand, and apparently in perfect condition. Nevertheless, I started her engine, let it idle, revved it up, and shut it down before the disturbance might excite undue notice. Having seen that her fuel tanks were full, I checked the weight of the jerrycans neatly and properly lashed down alongside one of the lockers in the well-deck. Their heft told me both were full, but I unsnapped the caps and smelled the contents. Petrol beyond all doubt.

And so, all right. So far as I could tell, the boat was perfectly okay. I locked her up and walked back to the Maritim and got into the car without succumbing to a strong temptation to enter the hotel and have one more quiet drink at the bar. I checked and double-checked all the miles back to Lübeck. Nobody was following me.

*     *     *

'So what's the verdict?' Edna said.

Charlie was garaging the car.

'The boat looks fine, but I'm still a bit worried.'

'What about?' Edna said.

'This business of it being only three-and-three.'

'That's the deal,' she said. 'Three of us, and three of them.'

'Edna, are you sure?'

'Farrow, how can one ever be sure?'

The room seemed oppressively hot. I loosened my collar and pulled down my tie.

'How's Dorf?'

'Still sleeping,' she said.

'Blessed are those who know not.'

'A philosopher, yet!' Edna said, and it was then that I got the first inkling.

'Are you Jewish, Edna?' I said.

'Why do you ask? Does it matter?'

'Of course not. Not in the least.'

'I wouldn't want to think you were patronising me.'

'Do me a favour,' I said, 'I just wish to Christ I was big enough!'

133

She threw back her head to laugh, and opened her handbag to grope for a cigar. 'Farrow, you're a flatterer,' she said.

'And you,' I said, 'are a lovely lady.'

'Are you propositioning me now?'

'Would that this were the time, and place.'

'And a poet, already!' she said.

'So marry me, Edna.'

'You smooth-talking rascal!'

'Is it yes, or no?'

'It's a definite no.'

'But when a lady says "no", she means "maybe" . . .'

'. . . and by "maybe", she always means "yes".'

As we were laughing, Charlie came back from putting the car away. He resumed his seat, and straightened his trousers, and hauled out a clean handkerchief prior to commencing his nostrils routine.

'What's so funny?' he said.

'Edna was telling me the one about the milkman.'

'You've heard it before,' Charlie said.

'No, that was the one *I* told *Edna*.'

'Well, when you're both settled,' he said, 'we'll talk about tomorrow.'

Edna wiped tears from her eyes, and after one last little chuckle, looked at me and said: 'Charles is right.'

'Oh, sure as hell. Never known to be wrong,' I said.

# SATURDAY

The morning which followed dawned fine and clear. Limitless hard blue skies feathered on high with herring-bone patterns of cirrocumulus. The surface of the sea was disturbed by nothing more ominous than a long but gentle swell. Here and there a lacing of whitecap, but no fretful tossing of spume. Nothing to augur impending change. But I had seen the sea adopt violent contortions well within the space of one hour, and the wind smelled fresh, and freshening . . .

'What do you think?' Edna said.

We were standing on the Strand at Travemünde, her shoulder about a foot below mine. She seemed so frail and tiny. Charlie was back at the house in Lübeck, looking after Dorf. The time was half past seven in the morning. I hunched in the carapace of my coat with my fists bunched deep in its pockets.

'It looks all right, now,' I said, 'but in two or three hours . . . you never can tell.'

'The weather forecast was good.'

'Believe the weather forecasts, you'll believe about anything.'

'Yes, I know,' Edna said, and a small hand stole into my raincoat pocket to link fingers with my own, 'but I feel I can trust your judgement, Farrow.'

'I can't think why,' I said. 'After all, you hardly know me.'

'Oh, but I *do*,' she said.

'What's that you've got in your handbag?' I could feel it pressing hard against my thigh.

'In my handbag? Probably my lipstick.'

'You must have big lips, then,' I said.

'Tell me, do you ever use lipstick?'

'Well, not lately. Why?'

'I've brought one for you. It's in the car.'

'What colour is it?' I said.

\*        \*        \*

135

That early morning reconnaissance on the Travemünde Strand was reviewed when we got back to Lübeck shortly before eight o'clock. Edna and I—she had done all the driving—were back again at the house barely an hour after she'd picked me up, when Charlie was taking his bath. Now, he was laved and shaved and dressed.

'Well, what about it?' he said.

Edna and I were shedding our coats. 'Weather-wise,' I said, 'there seems to be no problem. Where's Dorf?'

'Never mind Dorf,' Charlie said.

Edna said 'Right, then, who's for breakfast?'

'What a splendid idea,' I said. 'Edna, you think of everything.'

'One does one's best,' she said.

When I dropped my raincoat onto the sofa it fell with a muffled thud, because one of its pockets hid a magnum revolver, Smith & Wesson .357. I loved it so much I could have eaten it. I knew Charlie still had the Colt's, and that Edna had her heavy lipstick. All we needed now was a couple of automatic rifles.

'We could use some more fire-power,' I said.

Edna chose that moment to leave us. 'Well, talk amongst yourselves.'

When she was gone to the kitchen, 'So you're satisfied then?' Charlie said.

'I told you—so far as the weather's concerned.'

He blew, and reamed out, his nose, then used a second clean handkerchief to polish his rimless specs. I suffered the familiar performance in silence. I knew the futility of trying to proscribe, or interrupt it. He resettled his glasses on his nose, stowed away the used hankies, and straightened the hang of his clothes.

'Are you sure?'

'Jesus, Charlie, nothing's sure! And as I said before, we could do with some decent artillery.'

'Some decent *what*?' he said.

He knew quite well what I was talking about. This was just his way of giving himself time to think, and respond.

'Hey, come on!' I said.

136

'There's an Uzi Madsen on top of my wardrobe.'

'So *now* he tells me!' I said. 'Where did it come from?'

'You don't need to know. It's for use in emergency.'

'*Emergency?* You know bloodywell—!'

'I know nothing of the kind. To all intents and purposes we're conducting a simple exchange in a proper, civilised manner.'

'Do you really believe that?'

'No. But we're bound to proceed on that premise.'

'Do you trust the bastards?'

'No. But that's the way we're supposed to play it, and unless or until they try something naughty, that's how it's going to be.'

'How many magazines for the Uzi?'

'Half a dozen.'

'That all?'

'If it comes to a point we need more than six . . .'

'Don't tell me. I don't want to know.'

\*     \*     \*

The ways of women are multifarious. We owe our origins to them, and in so many ways, our continued existence. In the space of not much time, Edna created breakfast for four. Large helpings of sausages and eggs, the latter served up on crisply-fried bread.

'Go and get Dorf,' Charlie said.

Dorf was still chained to the airing cupboard, and apparently resigned to his fate. I had taken him for a pee in the early morning, when Edna came to pick me up, but it was patently obvious that his lordship in no way shared my concern. Charlie had risen, and taken his bath, leaving Dorf to lie in his sweat. I freed the cuff from the water pipe and led him along to the loo and held the loose shackle in my fist as he once again had a pee. As his water streamed into the bowl, 'Your friend is a monster,' he said.

'Never mind. Just shake your willy, and put it away,' I said, 'and we'll go downstairs and get some food.'

'A monster!'

'Shut up,' I said. 'If you want to eat, behave yourself.'

137

'What does it matter?' Dorf said.

*The condemned man ate a hearty breakfast.* I wondered for the umpteenth time what the hell I was doing in that place. Then, I remembered McKenzie, and 'Zip yourself up,' I said.

Dorf put me in mind of a big shambling bear controlled by a ring through its nose. His fleshy face was bewhiskered by a heavy two-days' growth, and his ill-fitting clothes were permeated by a pungent animal smell composed of sweat and dried vomit. His flabby grey cheeks appeared to be concave, collapsed upon themselves, and his sunken eyes were dull and opaque, bereft of the spark of life. As I made him precede me down the narrow staircase I was seized yet again by doubt in regard to the whole hellish enterprise. Dorf—that was not his real name—was, after all, just a fellow human being ensnared in that monstrous game the euphemism for which is Politics.

'Get him sat down,' Charlie said.

When I shepherded Dorf down onto the sofa he held up his free right hand in mute acceptance of the inevitable. As I linked his wrists, I said to Charlie:

'Now we can relax.'

My sarcasm was lost. He looked to Edna.

'What about the grub, then?'

'Ready when you are,' she said.

She was wearing a plastic pinafore to protect her clothes from hot fat, and its garish motif was cruelly incongruous: EAT AND BE MERRY it said.

\*       \*       \*

Charlie decreed that we pack up our bags and stow them all in the car before we quit the house in Lübeck, and I was not sorry to leave. I hoped I might never see it again. Nothing wrong with the house, but its ambience was plagued by mental associations I would very much rather eschew. The time on that bright November morning would have been about ten o'clock. I drove the BMW, with Charlie and Dorf in the back, and Edna followed us in her VW Golf. In that off-season period we experienced no problem at all in finding a legal parking space not too far from where the *Olga* was berthed. When Edna pulled up alongside us:

'How far to the boat?' Charlie said.

'Do you want it in yards, or metres?'

'Don't bugger about,' he said.

'All right, maybe a hundred yards.'

'Take a stroll, then.'

'Roger,' I said.

Inspired by a desire to go on living, I did my absolute best. I strolled up and down that waterfront with my eyes on *everything*, and when I was sure as sure can be:

'We seem to be clean,' I said. I was leaning on the cill of the open side-window of the BMW. 'Looks like we fooled the buggers.'

'What d'you mean *we*?' he said.

Edna stepped out of her little car, and without a glance at us, she locked the door and walked away.

'Where's Edna going?' I said.

'She's going to make a telephone call.'

'Where to?'

'Where do you think?'

'Christ,' I said, 'it's like pulling teeth!'

'Go run a check on the boat, and then get back here. Take the hardware.'

'Okay.'

The Uzi, together with its magazines, was encased in a plastic sleeve such as those used to carry fishing gear. I hauled it out of the open window and carried it by its sling down the waterside steps and onto the boat. In daylight, the *Olga* looked great. The winter sun struck glints off her brightwork and enhanced her well-scrubbed decks and created, on the moving water, a dappled reflection of her hull. I unlocked and opened the solid teak hatch and stepped down into the saloon, and laid the Uzi on the starboard bench-bunk. All seemed quite serene, and it took me fewer than five minutes to satisfy myself that the boat was exactly as last I had checked her. When I returned to the car, Edna was sitting in the back beside Dorf, with Charlie on Dorf's other side, and I said:

'You look like the three wise monkeys.'

'Never mind the wit,' Charlie said. 'Any sign of anything?'

'Not one jot or tittle,' I said. 'I'd say we're running free and clear.'

It would certainly have seemed that way. There was no undue movement along the Strand, just a normal to-and-fro with the usual activity of messing about in boats. There was always a chance, of course, that some of those who were messing about might not be so innocent as they seemed, but we were three professionals and if with our combined skills we could not discern any special interest . . .

'That's it, then. Let's go,' Charlie said.

Dorf was powerless to put a spoke in the wheel. He never had the slightest chance. When Charlie pulled him out of the car with their wrists linked right to left, Edna walked close on Dorf's right side and we boarded the boat in a bunch. With the four of us safely ensconced below decks, 'Farrow, do your stuff,' Charlie said.

I looked to Edna. 'You got the co-ordinates?'

'Never mind,' Charlie said, 'just get this bloody thing out of here.'

'I need some help with the warps.'

'No you don't. Get on with it.'

'I think you might manage,' Edna said.

'Thank you, Edna. Thanks very much.'

'Not at all, you're welcome,' she said.

She was right, of course. There was no great problem. I cast off fore and aft and stepped back on board without difficulty, but I couldn't help feeling miffed that neither of the buggers had offered to help. As I took us out down-channel I wondered idly, not that it mattered very much, if the *Olga*'s owners had a permanent berth or whether, when we returned, it might have been taken by a visiting craft. A subconscious device of the id, against the fear of never returning. When we reached the open sea, I had never known the Baltic be so tranquil. I had seen it extremely rough, and I'd seen it icebound many miles offshore, but today was a perfect day for heaving-to and coming alongside another wallowing boat. We had enjoyed the benefit of an outgoing tide and the steady following sea had

140

nursed us out into deep blue water with never so much as a splash over bows or gunnels or counter. It felt good to have a wheel in my hands, and had it not been for the doubts which plagued me, I might well have enjoyed the trip.

But what is the gulf between duty, and reason; sense, and sensibility? What quirk of the human condition permits such delusion of ourselves? Might it be a yearning for the innocence of childhood? We were all of us keenly aware that our aim to swap Dorf for McKenzie was like trying to sell stolen goods to an incorruptible policeman. There could never have been any hope of our making the trade in a 'civilised manner'. The Others knew perfectly well that even by tacit Business standards, all protocol had gone by the board when we stole our man from the Cousins, and even were the Section a recognised agency—such as MI5 or 6—the operation would still be *sub rosa*, and *sub rosa* means anything goes. No rules, no names, no pack-drill. That which cannot be seen to have happened incites no penalties, because neither protagonist needs to admit of having had cognizance.

As I voiced these thoughts to Charlie when he emerged from down below, he was gazing all around an empty sea. We were twenty-odd miles offshore, and heading due north towards somewhere in Sweden with never another vessel in sight. Not even a ferry, or a fishing boat. The Baltic seemed eerily still. We were rolling slightly, and gently pitching, but the movement was hardly so much as to trouble the most queasy of landlubbers.

'. . . the calm before the storm,' I said.

'Think positive, Farrow.'

'I *am* thinking positive.' I had throttled back to three knots, barely enough to maintain leeway, and the *Olga*'s bows rose and dipped with an almost swan-like motion. 'Maybe they're not going to come.'

'They'll come, all right.'

'So how do they find us, with no co-ordinates?'

'They'll find us.'

'How? By satellite?'

'Don't get technical. Go downstairs, and check the Uzi.'

'*Downstairs?* Bloody hell!'

141

'I told you not to get technical. How do I drive this thing?'

'Just take the wheel, and hold it steady.'

'Right. Get on with it, then.'

Edna was sitting on the starboard side, smoking a thin cigar. Dorf, oblivious and uncaring, was lying flat on his back, staring dumbly at the deck-head which was just a fraction too low for me to stand completely upright, so I sat beside Edna and said:

'Charlie says to check the Uzi.'

'You don't need to bother,' she said. 'Do you suppose I'd buy a pig in a poke?'

'Oh, so *you* bought it?' I said.

'Did you think it was a present from Santa Claus?'

'Edna, you're a cracker,' I said.

When I unzipped the fishing sleeve the cabin was suddenly filled with the distinctive odour of Three-in-One oil. A very evocative smell, and one which, in this case, was curiously reassuring. There is no smell on earth which nearly resembles the smell of a well-kept gun. Edna watched as I examined the weapon, and checked the magazines. I was pleased to see they were of the type which carried forty rounds, and not the smaller thirty-rounds version. With the Uzi's cyclic rate of six hundred rounds per minute, the difference might appear small, but it's often such tiny differences . . .

I extended the metal folding stock, loaded and cocked the gun, and laid it on the mid-section table. Then, I lined up the magazines, so that each was immediately ready to hand.

'Do you know how to use this thing?'

'Don't teach your granny how to suck eggs.'

'Just asking, Edna,' I said.

'There is a time for every purpose.'

'Ecclesiastes—right?'

'Farrow, I do believe you've read a few books.'

'Well, I've read *that* one,' I said.

\*       \*       \*

The Others were playing cat and mouse. We wallowed on the swell, barely making headway, over the next two hours.

They might of course have had problems far beyond our ken, but I didn't believe it, and neither did Charlie.

'They're buggering us about,' he said. 'I'll kill that big fat bastard!'

He was talking about Herr Schwenk.

'Come on, he's only a go-between, Charlie.'

'I'll still kill the swine!' he said.

'Well, before you get too excited, look out to starboard,' I said.

'Starboard? What's starboard?'

'Right-hand side. In this case, out to the east.'

No more than a suddenly-appearing shape, but definitely a boat, and one which soon proved fast-approaching.

'What d'you make of it?' Charlie said.

'In the absence of any other, I'd say it must be Them.'

'All right, so listen, Farrow—'

'What's it look like I'm doing?' I said.

'Don't let the bastards get too close.'

'What d'you mean by "close"?'

'Thirty, forty yards at most.'

'So how do we make the swap?'

'Life-line, and life-jacket. Got it?'

'No.'

'Jesus Christ!' Charlie said. 'Do I have to spell it out for you?'

'Yes. And you've got about ten minutes,' I said.

'Right, so pin your cauliflower ears back—'

'Make that shell-like,' I said.

\*     \*     \*

'All right, Farrow. What do you think?'

'Could be, it's hard to tell.'

'Look, you're the bloody expert! Is it faster than ours, or not?'

'I'm telling you, Charlie, I just don't know.'

'Jesus Christ!' he said.

She was about the same length as the *Olga*, and of a similar type, but I had no way of knowing the size of her engine, and it might have been powering twin screws.

143

Somewhat unlikely, but possible. I couldn't make a guess from her wake, because the boat had reduced speed and was approaching bows-on. The closing had taken them twenty minutes, and it hadn't been a minute too long. In the meantime, we had all been busy. Charlie had worked out a plan.

Edna got the heartbreaking job of forcing open the booze locker and bringing the bottles up top and emptying their contents over the side. As she performed this sacrilege, I was filling each empty in turn with petrol from one of the spare jerrycans. Charlie's sacrifice was much more personal. He was ripping up his handkerchiefs to make wicks for Molotov cocktails and now, as the two boats closed, there were nine such devices neatly lined up on the port-side locker top, their necks out of sight just under the bulwarks. By this time, the well-deck stank of expensive liquor and petrol fumes. As did all of us.

'Right then, Farrow, you know what to do.'

What I had to do was to handle the *Olga* like a rank amateur, like a man whose experience of the sea had been confined to rolling up his trousers and getting his ankles wet. It might just work. It had better work. The thing which worried me was that to make it seem *so* clumsy might require rather more skill than that of which I was capable. Nothing to do but to try.

The perfect conditions were working against me. A rough and choppy sea would have made the deception much more credible. As it was, my erstwhile skills were taxed to the utmost limit. Almost any bloody fool who is able to drive a motor car can handle a good boat in calm seas, because a wheel is a wheel, and a throttle is a throttle and left and right, too, are the same. When the boats had drawn within hailing distance, roughly thirty yards, Charlie said:

'Stop. Put the handbrake on.'

When I snatched the throttle back, and threw the drive into neutral the *Olga* sank on her bows and began, very gently, to wallow. The Others, loosely alongside, might almost have been a mirror-image. Very similar craft, each with two men astern on their well-decks, the cabin side-screens opaque. Here, aboard us, two others: Edna and

144

Dorf down below in our cabin, and if the Others were observing the rules, McKenzie and one more minder in theirs. The slight breeze was from the north-east, and I thanked my stars that the stench of petrol which seemed to envelop us was being wafted away from them. I just hoped that Edna's cigarette lighter would work, as usual, first time.

Charlie cupped his hands around his mouth, and shouted:

'Bring up our man!'

One of the men on the other boat nodded to his buddy-boy, who turned to the hatch and mouthed an instruction. Then, he called: 'Now produce ours!'

Charlie spoke down to Edna. 'Let's have the laddo out here.'

There was movement at the open hatch and Dorf emerged from below and stood, submissive, between us. Again in weird mirror-image, there appeared on the other boat a very familiar figure.

'Jock! Are you all right?' I yelled.

Charlie murmured, 'Steady, you pillock.'

But I perceived a nod from young Jock, and the smile on his face put fresh heart in me.

'Just get it right,' Charlie said.

What he meant was that I should not forget the strictures of his scheme. From now on, timing was vital. The boats were drifting on the swell, roughly parallel, and thirty yards apart. The air out at sea was quite cold, but I suddenly felt myself sweating.

'Handcuffs off!' Charlie yelled. Then, *sotto voce*, 'Watch the bastards.'

As he took the handcuffs off Dorf, the Others were taking the cuffs off McKenzie.

'It is done! Now, come alongside!'

I am paraphrasing, but such was the gist.

'Right. Do your stuff,' Charlie said.

Deliberately, I made all the wrong moves. I put on much too much power, and swung the wheel too far and too fast. With a boiling wake under our stern, I narrowly averted a disastrous collision when we cut across the other boat's

145

bows, and as Dorf and Charlie grabbed for holds on the rail:

'Jesus Christ, Farrow!' he said. 'That just about scared the shit out of me!'

'You and me both,' I said.

But truth to tell, I was exhilarated. This was my kind of thing. Bracing myself, I spun the wheel to bring us hard over to port, and Dorf and Charlie were thrown against each other. Once our wake had described a wide arc, we were coming at the others bows-on, with theirs facing seawards and us with our stem straight in line with the shore.

With his left hand clutched around the rail, 'Have you got it right?' Charlie said.

'You'd better believe it. How's Edna?'

'Never mind Edna,' he said, 'are you bloody sure you know what you're doing?'

'So far, so good,' I said. 'On our next attempt, we'll be stem-to-stern.'

'I want us front-to-back, with our front end pointing straight towards land.'

'That's *exactly* what I've just said!'

I made a nonsense of our second approach, almost ramming the Others bows-on, and my next fake move was to rush astern wildly and much too far, so that then I was forced to come ahead again. The object of all this incompetence was to lead the Others to believe that I was totally incapable of properly handling the craft. Eventually, with both boats hove-to some thirty-odd yards apart, Charlie waved his arms.

'It's no good! It'll have to be life-lines and jackets!'

'My God! I can't swim!' Dorf cried.

Charlie said 'Well, then, you'd better put this on.'

Dorf's hands were shaking so much he was hardly able to loop the ties. As Charlie lent him a hand, I watched a similar operation over on the other boat, and wondered why the Others had complied. I wondered why they hadn't insisted that we stay right where we were, and leave them to do the manoeuvring. The notion gave pause for grim thought. It suggested they didn't care *what* we did. However, I was comforted to note that Jock needed no help with the life-saver. He donned the jacket himself, and it looked as

146

though he was fastening it properly. Then, he tied his own line around his chest, nice and close, well up under the armpits. I had enough faith in the lad to believe he would know the importance of making a good firm knot. I just prayed that the Others had not tampered with the rope, perhaps cut it half-way through, because all now depended on their not having done so. Not really likely, of course, because they'd been expecting a deck-to-deck transfer.

Our own line lay coiled and ready. Charlie tied one end around Dorf, and heaved the loops across the water. His first throw fell just short, but the Others' effort was accurate. The back-spliced tail of their rope almost lashed me across the face. I put up a hand to grab, and my fingers caught hold, and I hauled in the slack. Charlie was retrieving his line, and when he had recovered the dripping coils he poised and heaved again and the extra weight of the waterlogged line carried it across the gap which separated the rolling boats. As the Others were dragging it in—we had purposely put on far too much—Charlie said:

'All set, Farrow?'

'In a minute,' I said. I was hastily making fast the line which linked young McKenzie to us, throwing a double-hitch around one of the port-side stanchions. Soon as my hands were free, I jumped back to the wheel and said, 'Ready now, Charlie.'

'Right, let's go then,' he said.

After which, everything happened at once. Even had I been able to take note, there would have been no time for real comprehension. As it was, my only concern was to pile on the knots and pile them on fast. The *Olga* performed beautifully. She responded like a thoroughbred when I opened the throttle wide, and I felt the surge of power and her bows rise up as the screw took hold. With one fast backwards glance, I yelled:

'Okay, Charlie?'

'Keep going!'

That which had happened was this: when Charlie toppled Dorf into the sea, McKenzie jumped overboard and so was being towed astern of us, bouncing on the roil of our wake and doubtless collecting multiple bruises. At one and

147

the very same time, my eardrums were pounded by the hellish clatter of automatic weapons fire. Some of ours, mostly theirs. I could hear above the roar of *Olga*'s engine the ongoing splintering crash as her port-side side-screens were shattered, and the answering thunder from below as Edna opened up with the Uzi. The harsh staccato rattling was punctuated by heavy booms as Charlie let loose with the Colt's .45. There was a burst of stuttering thuds as bullets stitched a pattern of holes in our hull. Then the shooting stopped abruptly, and suddenly there was no other noise but that of the engine and the fierce rush of water streaming along the hull. I locked us on course at full ahead and stooped to lean into the hatch. The cabin was hazy with gunsmoke, and filled with an acrid smell from the fumes of exploded powder. As Edna looked up at me, slipstream through the shattered side-screens ruffled her short grey hair. All of this in the space of one minute.

'You okay, Edna?'

'Yes. What about Charles, and Hector?'

'Charlie's all right,' I said, 'and we're going to get Jock inboard.'

'Can they catch us up?'

'I don't know. But if they do, keep your head down.'

'I'll make them keep theirs down,' she said.

Charlie was watching the other boat, now a full quarter-mile astern, as she heeled hard over in a full-speed turn.

'Stand by to get Jock in!' I bawled. 'He must be damn-near drowned!'

We were dragging him at close on thirty knots through a furious boiling wake which snatched and slapped at his body, tossing it into the air then burying it half-seas under.

'Right! Let's make it fast!' Charlie yelled.

I grabbed at the throttle and yanked it full back and paused not long enough before engaging slow astern. When the juddering screw began to do battle with our forward momentum the *Olga* shook in every frame, and it was some fraught seconds before she began to respond. The instant she settled down, I threw the gear into neutral and scrambled to give Charlie a hand. We hauled young Jock close into the side and leaned down over the rail to grab at

148

his jacket and heave him over. It took all of our combined strengths. Totally helpless, bruised and battered, his body was a limp dead weight. We heaved him inboard, choking and retching, and laid him like some huge landed fish among the bottles rolling around in the well-deck.

'Are you all right, Jock?' I said.

He couldn't speak, he could barely nod. But he mustered the ghost of a smile, and Charlie punched me hard on the thigh.

'Come on, get us moving!' he said.

I saw as I thrust the throttle open that the seas had nudged us slightly off course, and I made the correction before switching to auto. Charlie, helped by Edna, was struggling to move Jock below into the comparative safety of the cabin. As the *Olga* got into her stride, I looked back to see what the Others were doing.

They had gained a lot of sea. God only knew what was happening to Dorf; the poor wretch was probably drowned. Had his buddies had the humanity to heave-to and take him on board, the delay would have given us more of an edge. As it was, all we could hope was that the drag of his body might slow them a fraction. Charlie came back up on deck, and checked the magazine of his pistol. As he slotted it back into the butt, he turned around towards our pursuers.

'They're chasing us.'

'No shit?'

'Are they going to catch up?'

'Who knows?'

'Can't you tell, you daft bugger?'

'Not just yet,' I said. 'We stopped for a while—remember?'

'How far have we got to go before the bastards are forced to give over?'

'I reckon about fifteen miles.'

'What's our speed?'

'Around thirty knots.'

'So what's that in terms of time?'

'Twenty, twenty-five minutes.'

'Christ! Is there nothing more you can do?'

'Not a thing, we're going flat-out.'

'Right. Let the buggers come, then,' he said. He pocketed the Colt's, and began to gather up his Molotov cocktails, lining them up once again on top of the port-side locker. 'Just make sure they come up on this side.'

* * *

'Yes, I reckon they can do it, Charlie.'

'Made your mind up, now, have you?' he said.

'Well, we're both at top speed, and they're gaining.'

'How much longer, then?'

'Maybe seven or eight minutes.'

'Shouldn't you be driving this thing?'

'No need at the moment, not 'til the fun starts. I'll go take a look at Jock.'

He was lying on the starboard bunk-bench with his head hanging over the edge, sicking up gobs of briny slime. Edna was crouched by his side, holding one of his hands in both of her own.

'How's he doing?' I said.

She looked up and nodded. 'He's going to be all right. What's the score up there?'

'How many full magazines you got left?'

'So it's like that, is it?' she said. 'How long before—?'

'Not much more than five minutes. How many magazines?'

'Two full, plus about a half of one.'

'Better take this, then,' I said. I handed her the .357.

'Don't you like my lipstick?'

'It's more use down here,' I said, 'and when the fireworks start, I'm going to be busy.'

'Shouldn't Hector be lying on the floor?'

'Good thinking Edna—come on, you young rascal, let's have you down on the deck.'

He must have been a mass of contusions, and possibly had a few cracked ribs, and was obviously suffering agonies. He groaned as we eased him off the bunk, and spewed up another dribble of salt water. 'That's the way, get it all off your chest—put a cushion under him, Edna.' As she raised his head, he opened his eyes and tried to speak.

150

'Look at him,' I said, 'there's nothing ails the young bugger. He's malingering again!' Then, 'Just relax, Jock. It's going to be okay.'

'Any special drill?' Edna said.

'Conserve your ammo. Don't start shooting until they're fully alongside, then open up with all you've got.'

'Make 'em keep their heads down?'

'That's right. Don't attempt individual targets, just pour it on fast as you can. If it isn't all over in about half a minute . . .'

'Farrow, say no more.'

'See you anon, then.'

'Bet your boots.'

What a fabulous old dame.

'FARROW!'

'Coming, Charlie!'

When I stepped out on deck, he was dipping one end of a length of rope into the neck of a jerrycan. His purpose, patently obvious, gave me a twinge of alarm.

'Better watch what you're doing with that, ole buddy.'

'Never mind the advice, lend a hand.'

We emptied about half of the petrol from each of the jerrycans, sloshing the fuel over the side. Then we secured the caps, and tied the cans together with rope, lashing them as close as we could. It was a struggle to get them up onto the coach-roof, but from there just one mighty shove would topple the whole shebang overboard. A potential floating bomb.

'If they hit this lot before we ditch 'em, it's Goodbye Vienna,' I said.

'You just attend to the driving.'

I turned to look astern. The other boat had loomed much larger. She was coming on not very fast, but implacably sure and steady. I was thankful for the fact that the speed at which we were forging ahead in an almost dead-calm sea afforded us maximum stability. Just a long smooth pitch, and no roll. I experienced a feeling of inadequacy. At that moment, there was nothing I could do except place my trust in Charlie.

And *there* was another thing. In the hectic events of the

previous few days I had seldom reminded myself that Charlie's not-so-old injuries had to be plaguing him. He was capable of thrusting them out of his mind, but the body is something quite else: it can be driven to great lengths, but a final breakdown comes as inevitable.

'That's just about the lot.' He wiped his hands down the front of his Burberry and hauled out the big Colt's gun and checked, again, there was one up the spout. 'Three left. How's Edna?'

'Okay. She's got about a hundred rounds.'

'How's McKenzie?'

'He'll live.'

He produced Edna's lighter, and thumbed the wheel, and flame sprang up first time.

'Look at that. Lovely. We're home and dry.'

'Here they come,' I said.

I was standing at the wheel with one hand on the throttle, twisting from the waist to look back and keep a check on the action. The other boat was drawing close, about forty yards off our port quarter. Any split-second now they were going to cut loose with a hail of fire.

'Now, Charlie, NOW!' I bawled.

I don't think he heard me, but it didn't matter. Even as the shout left my throat, he bundled the jerrycans over the side and the Others opened up. They must have had two, maybe three machine pistols. But in all that shattering din, he was calmly aiming the big Colt's gun with both hands gripping the butt and the three booming shots, so close to my ear, seemed to merge into one huge roar. It all seemed to happen in the proverbial slow-motion and over and above, a great roaring *whoosh* as the jerrycans exploded in a great burst of smoke and fire. Charlie flung himself down behind the cabin bulkhead and scrambled on hands and knees to get at the Molotov cocktails. As he snatched up his petrol-soaked rope and flicked Edna's cigarette lighter, 'Put the brakes on!' he yelled.

When I shut off all power the *Olga* ploughed on, but the overall effect was that the Others ploughed on that much faster through a blinding curtain of flames, and they were running alongside before they knew it. There was a thunderous barrage from below as Edna let go with the Uzi. I was spinning the wheel to keep us up close to the maelstrom, so that Charlie could do his thing. He was hurling those primitive missiles as fast as he could snatch them, and throw. The first of his flaming bottles glanced off the other boat's bows, but others struck true and smashed through side-screens to explode with such hellish force as to blow off the coach-roof and fling blazing debris all over the smoke-filled sky. In the small meantime we were falling astern as they forged helplessly ahead, encompassed in a great ball of fire. Some nights, I still hear the screams.

*    *    *

Alas, poor Dorf. We checked that he was dead, and left his body afloat to be washed on the beach by the incoming tide. Callous? What else could we do? We needed to get ashore, and away, before Officialdom arrived on the scene.

# LATER

A tiny hamlet lost in the Cotswolds, forgotten since the Domesday Book. The church was early Norman, a perfect little gem steeped in the sanctity of ancient stones hallowed by a millennium of prayer. The tall gnarled yews which enclosed its graveyard—some hundreds of years less old, and doubtless planted to yield staves for longbows— remained as-ever green, but the grove of elms was stark and gaunt and its colony of rooks wheeled about its bare black branches cawing dolefully. Their harsh sad cries seemed appropriate to that dismal January day.

There was later to be a memorial service at St Clement Danes in the Strand, but the actual interment was strictly private. Family only, no flowers. So apart from young Jock, and maybe Edna, it was obvious that the Man had outlived all of his progeny. *Sic transit gloria*. The only other person with them in the foremost left-side pew was the omnipresent Miss Hetherington, recognisable from the back in spite of the heavy coat she was wearing, and the pew up there at front-right was occupied by three men and two women all of them far from young. Possibly, probably, old family retainers. These eight mourners aside, Charlie and me were the only others. I was half-expecting to have seen representatives of the Section, from Scotland and from the south, but it seemed that we were special.

And, after all, why not?

The church was pervaded by a deathly chill. It was colder inside than out, and a pale winter sun served only to emphasise the icy blues of stained glass. The adzed-oak coffin, unadorned by blooms, and resting on plain trestles in the aisle seemed a fitting and proper receptacle for those earthly remains of a man whose tenets had always been pure and simple. He had loved this Sceptred Isle with a passion beyond all doubt, or question.

We had arrived deliberately late, and had slipped into a pew near the back with the eulogy already begun. Charlie had picked me up early that morning, and we'd driven

154

down from the north with a stop for a sandwich at a pub near Cheltenham. I had not wanted to come, but Charlie had insisted. Now, as the parson droned on, I shivered in my overcoat and whispered:

'Jesus, Charlie! It's cold!'

He elbowed me very hard in the ribs and hissed:

'Belt up! Show respect!'

The vicar appeared to be a recent incumbent with no personal knowledge of the deceased. Too, he was suffering from a heavy cold. He kept wiping the drip off his nose with a handkerchief plucked from the sleeve of his surplice, and it was evident that all he desired was to do his duty and get back to the manse in front of a nice warm fire. Far from feeling affronted, I empathised with the youth.

It was snowing when we gathered at the graveside. Nothing very fierce, just big soft wafers falling slow and gentle, but the wetness on my face was a trifle too warm to be caused by snowflakes. The service at last reached its end.

*Ashes to ashes, and dust to dust . . .*

'That's it, then. Let's go,' Charlie said.

We were the first of that small sad gathering to turn and move away, but as we reached the lych-gate we were overtaken by Jock, who eased between us and grasped our arms.

'I say! You're not going!' he said. 'I want you both to come back to the house!'

'Very nice of you,' Charlie said, 'but it's a long hard drive, and we have to get back.'

'No, no!' young McKenzie said. 'There's masses of room, you can stay overnight.' He half-turned to look down the lane, where Edna and Miss Hetherington were being ushered into a Rolls. 'Besides, you haven't said hello to Aunt Edna.'

Charlie disengaged his arm and gently, 'It's finished, lad,' he said. 'Know what I mean? It's all over.'

A mute appeal to me, but I knew in my heart that Charlie spoke true.

'That's right. He's right, Jock,' I said.

# EPILOGUE

Every month, regular as clockwork, the routine statement from my bank reflects a substantial credit. I know it has to derive from some kind of private trust fund set up by the Man, but I have never attempted to investigate the source.

*In Memoriam.*